HIDDEN

JAY .H. DEE

Cover Photos by Andrey Armyagov and Iakov Kalinin, from Depositphotos.
Cover design by Jay .H. Dee, Victoria, Australia.

Hidden

ISBN 978-0-9942436-6-9

Dedicated to Grandma and Grandad.
You two are permanent fixtures in my life,
beloved and steadfast.
I will always treasure your unconditional
love, your examples and your guidance.
I'm so grateful God gave me both of you!

ACKNOWLEDGEMENTS

Many thanks to my husband and daughter for allowing me to sit at the computer for hours finishing this book. Your tolerance for my penchant to disappear head and shoulders into a story has been hugely appreciated.

A special thanks to Yanina for your advice with cover design. Your encouragement has been invaluable.

Thanks also to my church family for your support in my journey, both personally and as an author. I feel so blessed to have been planted amongst you. May God continue to richly bless you all!

NAVY TERMINOLOGY

CO: Commanding Officer.

XO: Executive Officer.

The Bosun or boatswain: is an officer on a ship who is responsible for the rigging, anchors, cables, sails, and other errata that are used to keep a ship running smoothly. He or she is considered to be the foreman of the ship's crew, because this sailor issues orders to the deck crew.

The Coxswain: in the Navy, this is the driver of a small boat, and the senior petty officer on a small ship.

RHIB: Rigid-hulled Inflatable Boat. Each RHIB is 7.2-metres in length and is water jet propelled. Each RHIB is stored in a dedicated cradle and davit, and is capable of operating independently from the patrol boat as they carry their own communications, navigation, and safety equipment.

Crane: This lowers and lifts the RHIBs in and out of the water, from and into their cradle and davit.

Quarter deck: This is the deck space at the rear of the ship.

Bridge: The command centre in the ship.

Galley: The kitchen on board the boat.

Wardroom: a commissioned officers' mess (eating area) on board a warship.

Radar: a system for detecting the presence, direction,

distance, and speed of aircraft, ships, and other objects, by sending out pulses of radio waves which are reflected off the object back to the source.

EOD: Electrical Optical Device. This is used to view objects at long range.

FFV: Foreign fishing vessel.

PROLOGUE

1759, in the Dutch East Indies:

The loud report of a canon set the crew of The Hildegard on edge. Sailors above deck held a collective breath as the telltale hiss of a cannonball hurtling toward them joined the constant rhythm of waves breaking at the bow.

The Dutch galleon sliced easily through deep blue waters, yet not fast enough to outrun the Portuguese caravel bearing down upon them. The square sails on its bowsprit and front mast, and the triangular sails on her other three masts, billowed and caught every last gust of wind. Upon a large splash near the stern, the crew of The Hildegard exhaled in relief.

"That was close, Captain," bosun, Rado Caspar, remarked from his position at the rail.

Beside him, Captain Salomon Chan lowered his telescope, a dark scowl upon his heavily bearded face.

"Helmsman!" he barked. "Hard to starboard!" He glanced at Rado and a devilish gleam lit his brown eyes. "Wait until my order and then fire all four starboard cannons. We'll teach those brutes to plunder in our waters."

He returned his gaze to the Portuguese renegade

ship and raised the telescope to his right eye. The pirate vessel came easily into view now that The Hildegard was facing it side on. He had to time this just right or he might very well get his men killed. If the pirate vessel got off a shot first, the damage would be catastrophic.

Rado nervously watched the enemy ship turning into position in like manner. "Now sir?"

The captain's tone was calculating. "Not yet."

The Hildegard rocked the last few degrees so that her starboard side was completely exposed. The caravel was a split second behind in a similar manoeuvre. If its captain decided to fire now, it would all be over.

Salomon's keen eyes narrowed and the devilish sparkle returned. "Fire! Fire! Fire! Fire!"

The crew manning the canons below deck complied and the still sea air was rent by four successive blasts. Men lining the railing watched in anxious anticipation. If the shots missed, the next volley from the enemy ship would blow them out of the water. They waited. Salomon counted the seconds.

Suddenly three mighty explosions ripped open the pirate vessel from bow to stern, the fourth narrowly missing the ship. Rado's triumphant shout was one of over one-hundred. The captain's mouth quirked in a subdued smile. He had done what was necessary to protect his men and his boat.

"Helmsman," he called over the din of his celebratory crew, "ninety degrees to starboard. Let's go back and fish out the survivors."

"They might very well be laden with goods stolen from other ships in the Dutch East Indies. Spices, gold…" Rado let the tantalising thought dangle.

Salomon's mouth quirked in amusement. "How ironic. An explorer vessel plundering pirates."

Rado grinned and leapt into action, preparing his deckhands to board.

1

Present day:

A dark head breached the surface. A set of pearly white teeth gleamed in contrast to mellow brown skin as the young woman grinned. Nethania Brideson removed her diving goggles and her vivid blue eyes danced with delight. She glanced up at her assistant standing at the back of the boat. It was a trawler that had recently been converted for the purpose of marine studies.

"Padi, I saw a species of coral we thought had died off in the area. The colours were incredible! Get your diving gear and come see."

Padi Ato's expression was apologetic. "Not now Netania."

He too was a marine biologist. Due to his Japanese heritage, it was difficult to guess his age. He could be anywhere between twenty-five and forty.

"Captain say weadder turn bad."

Nethania frowned, her two shapely brows drawing together. "He doesn't want to head into port does he? We've only been out on the reef a couple of days. There's still so much to survey. We haven't even begun tagging-"

"Please Netania," he interrupted anxiously, his voice as respectful as always. "Captain say storm very big."

Nethania studied her colleague and her heart sank. They had worked hard to organise this voyage and source equipment and endorsements. They did not need more delays!

"Alright." She swam the last few metres to the boat. She hauled herself onto the lower ledge at the back and then over a thigh high railing onto the deck.

Padi's concerned expression broke with a sunshiny warm smile. He leant against the side. "Tell me about coral."

Nethania grinned and animatedly began a description. Padi seemed to revel in every detail, clearly loving their work as much as she did.

~

"Look at the size of that!"

Ollie Startori heard the excited exclamation as he came from the galley and through the wheelhouse with several cold cans of soft drink. He stepped into the sun and grinned at his deckhand helping their clients haul an enormous marlin from the water onto the charter boat.

Dayne glanced up from the fish now writhing on the deck and smiled broadly. "Not bad for his first catch." He gave the excited teenage boy and his proud father a wide grin.

"I reckon!" Ollie chuckled and handed each of the men a can. He held onto Dayne's while he did the dirty work and put the marlin out of its misery.

"What do you say? Shall we drink to your success?" Ollie opened his coke with a satisfying fizz.

Young Tony beamed with pride. His father's warm smile fell upon him. "I'll be in that." He popped open his can.

Dayne rose and wiped dirty hands on his shorts. He took the coke Ollie offered and raised it in salute with the others.

"To Tony!" Ollie declared.

"To Tony!" they all chimed in.

The boy's grin nearly split his face. The group took a long, cold swig.

"I can't wait to show mum," Tony enthused.

"She'll be surprised," Ethan assured his son. "She's always complaining I never bring anything home. Just wait till she sees what I caught."

Tony gave his teasing father a playful shove. "You mean, wait till she sees what *I* caught."

Ethan chuckled and passed Dayne and Ollie a cheeky smile. "It was worth a try."

Ollie thought he heard the crackle of the radio and excused himself to go and check. He entered through the doorway on the deck. Inside on the right was a cushioned bench seat. To the left, looking out the angled windows that provided a one-hundred and eighty degree view of the surrounding ocean, was the captain's chair before an inbuilt desk. The desk sported a computer screen used for radar and echo sounding, GPS, a compass, a radio, steering wheel and an accelerator lever.

A familiar voice came clearly over the radio. "Fishing vessel Dream Catcher, this is HMAS Hartfield, do you copy?"

Ollie smiled and picked up the receiver and keyed the microphone. "Yeah, copy that Jaffa. How are ya mate?"

"Ollie, is that you?" the voice returned in surprise.

"Sure is." He glanced at the radar screen and read the position of the Australian Armidale class patrol boat he had once served on as the boatswain's mate. They were roughly five kilometres away. "What are you guys up to out here?"

He had worked on The Hartfield a little over five years ago, until a bullet shattered his knee and he was assigned a shore posting. Loving life on the sea, Ollie had quit the navy not long after that and gone to work on a fishing charter out of Brisbane. A few years later his dream of owning and operating his own fishing adventure business became a reality.

"Keeping a lookout for poachers," Leading Seaman Jeffrey Williams, Jaffa to most, replied. "Seems we found one."

Ollie dropped into his chair at the helm. "Sorry to disappoint you Jaffa, just a marlin and a few Spanish mackerel."

"Wow, the marlin is a beauty! Who caught it? The kid or his dad who are both posing for a photograph?"

Ollie frowned. He glanced out the doorway onto the deck to find everything as his friend had described. He shook his head. "You're eyeballing us with the EOD aren't you?"

He was referring to the electrical optical device on the bridge of the patrol boat, which was able to view objects from kilometres away.

"Yep. Nice boat you've got there, although a little old. It looks like a 1990 Conquest."

Ollie half smiled in amusement. "It is. I can see you're putting your high tech equipment to good use."

Jaffa chuckled. "Affirmative."

Ollie leaned back in his chair and stretched his legs before him. His knee was aching, a clear sign the weather was going to cut up.

"Ollie, Navcom is giving us a severe storm warning. It looks to be about sea-state five or possibly worse. Suggest you head to port sometime soon."

Ollie exhaled loudly. Weather like that was sure to turn even Dayne green with seasickness. "Which direction is it coming from?"

"Northeast. Give it a couple of hours."

"Alright. We'll hightail it for Cairns. Thanks for the heads up."

"Anytime."

"Say hi to the guys for me and give them my sympathies. While you're all riding it out, I'll be home in port on solid ground. Over."

"Will do." Jaffa's tone was amused. "Over."

Ollie stood and replaced the radio handset. He surveyed the sky to the northeast through the slanted windows and was grateful for the warning. There did appear to be a storm brewing on the horizon.

He studied his charts spread on the desk beside the navigation equipment and plotted a direct course back to Cairns. He popped his head out the door to notify Dayne of the change in plans and then fired the engine and steered for home.

~

The Queen Maree bobbed about the ocean like a rubber ducky in a tumultuous bathtub. The creaky old trawler pitched downward and then its bow lurched up with the next six metre swell.

Nethania braced herself in the wheelhouse with her back against a wall, a hand to the adjacent closed door, and a foot against the cupboards at the end of the bench seat she was sitting on. Her stomach rolled right along with the boat and she kept her dinner down only by sheer willpower.

The skipper, a rough looking coot presumably in his fifties, sat at the helm and gripped the wheel with white knuckles. She and Padi knew him only as Macca, and neither marine biologist had seen him anything but laidback and cocky.

As Nethania glanced at his face for some indication of the status of their situation, she was unnerved to find him ashen.

"Where's the Jap?" he barked with only a brief look her way.

Nethania was too terrified to balk at his racist reference to her assistant. "Padi is below deck in his bunk." She watched an enormous swell rise from the ocean before them like a monster.

"Has he got a life jacket on?"

"We both do." She swallowed hard against the fear rising to choke her.

Macca grunted in acknowledgement and fought to keep the boat heading into the waves.

They had given up all hope of reaching port when the storm had hit full force. Instead Macca aimed his faithful rust bucket for the closer outcropping of tiny islands several hours from the Australian Coast. They were uninhabited due to their small size and their obscure location. However, Nethania hoped those islands just might be their salvation.

"Well get 'im up here! All we need is a rogue wave from the side an' we'll capsize. He'll never get out with a life jacket on if that happens."

Nethania dared not walk lest she tumble headlong into something and end up with a concussion. Instead she dropped to her knees and crawled to the narrow stairway between the helm and the rudimentary galley. It consisted of a couple of cupboards and a tiny stove and sink.

"Padi!" she hollered above the roar of the raging ocean outside. "The captain wants you up here!"

She received no response and squinted into the

darkness. She could just make out a form on one of the two bunks below.

"Padi, are you okay?"

He groaned miserably. "Feel bad!"

"Come up now!"

"I stay and die here."

Nethania could not resist a chuckle over his melodrama. "You're not going to die."

She carefully navigated the stairs and wove toward his bunk as though she had imbibed in too much wine. She grasped his arm and gave it a tug, realising as she did that he was clutching his backpack to his chest. She smiled momentarily in amusement until a nasty swell tossed her back, ramming her right hip hard against the stairs. She clenched her jaw to keep from crying out and quickly blinked back tears.

"Padi, now!"

She stumbled to his bunk and wrenched the pack from his grip. She then slung it over her arm and made for the steps. "Follow me!"

At the top of the stairs she gripped the cupboard with her left hand and the bench that was inbuilt with navigation equipment, with her right. She stepped into the wheelhouse.

She was about to turn and check that her assistant had followed, when the skipper cursed beside her. Nethania's worried gaze flew to his face and then out the window to their left where his stricken gaze was focused. She could see Macca's Adam's apple bob as he swallowed hard.

17

"I've lost control of the rudder!"

The boat bobbed parallel with a seven metre wave rising like a giant from the deep.

"Mayday! Mayday!" Macca spoke into the radio and braced for impact. "This is trawler Queen Maree at-"

The rogue wave lifted and rolled the boat before Macca had a chance to finish his call. Nethania let out a startled scream as she was tossed against the windows on the skipper's side of the wheelhouse. The trawler continued to roll until the boat was belly up and Nethania was lying on the roof.

Pressure from surrounding water caused the door to give way. Seawater quickly engulfed the wheelhouse in a roiling mass. Macca sloshed on foot for the open doorway and fought his way through the incoming deluge. Nethania floated up to the floor where there was now only a twenty centimetre pocket of air.

"Padi!" Panic accelerated her heart rate and threatened to choke her. "You've got to get out!"

Seawater gurgled higher until she had only five centimetres of oxygen between the floor and the water level. Nethania drew a deep breath, and with Padi's pack still looped over her arm, she grasped hold of the doorframe and pulled herself out. She kicked toward the surface.

Her foot caught on a loose piece of rigging and she slipped her shoe off. The buoyancy of her lifejacket took her the rest of the way. Her head cleared the surface and she gasped for breath. She frantically searched for the hull of the boat to cling to, but was swept away by another merciless wave.

She wondered as she fought for her life, if this was some kind of punishment for walking away from God all those months ago.

2

Lightning forked across a black stormy sky, and huge swells buffeted the patrol boat. Thankfully it was built to survive cyclonic weather up to sea state nine.

Executive officer, Lieutenant Lincoln Hobbs, grinned. Tonight they were pushing the Armidale class to her limit and he was loving every minute of it.

"Mayday! Mayday! This is trawler Queen Maree at-" The VHF transmission broke off, leaving only the sound of static on the bridge of The Hartfield.

"Queen Maree, this is HMAS Hartfield. Say again," leading seaman Jeffrey Williams responded over the radio.

Static was his only answer.

"Can you still see the trawler on radar?" Linc asked Lieutenant Ben Shepparton, the navigator.

Shep glanced sideways at the XO in the captain's chair. "Yes sir. She's at least an hour away."

Next to the executive officer at the controls was Leading Seaman Corrado Pugliese.

"Let's render assistance."

"Coz," Shep directed at the boatswains mate, "change our heading. Steer 035."

"Steering 035." Coz adjusted instrumentation.

"Wilko?" Linc called over his shoulder to the chief

engineer who was tucked away in an alcove at the rear of the bridge. Chief Petty Officer Jason Wilkinson was monitoring the engine statistics on a computer screen.

"Yes sir?"

"Can you give us anymore revs or am I asking a bit much of the girl in this weather?" Linc glanced back at the big, burly engineer who grinned.

"She's got more in 'er sir, you just haven't asked."

Linc smiled broadly and returned his gaze to the angry waves breaking over the bow. Spray from their vehement attack splashed against the windows and was swished aside by windscreen wipers. "Jaffa, give the captain a wakeup call."

Jaffa looked dubious. Lieutenant Commander Donnelly had looked exhausted when he left the bridge to catch a few winks of sleep less than an hour ago.

"Yes sir." He obediently flicked on the ship's intercom. He spoke into the receiver which looked much like a telephone. "Captain to the bridge."

~

"This is rather unorthodox sir." Chief Petty Officer Jay Lonigan helped the executive officer shoulder an air tank.

Linc grinned at the enormous bosun. "I can't let you blokes have all the fun."

Lon smiled in amusement while the XO and Able Seaman Tyson Rosetti pulled on flippers and masks.

The 7.2 metre water jet propelled Rigid Hulled Inflatable Boat rocked gently in the calm after the storm. At the controls was Coz. Petty Officer Farmer was at the bow with one hand on a metal handhold backing one of the inbuilt seats. He was awaiting the divers' findings.

Beside the RHIB, water lapped at the upturned hull of a damaged trawler. That it had remained afloat was a miracle. The sun peeked gingerly over the horizon to the east and cast a golden glow upon the ocean. It also provided visibility for the recovery mission.

"The odds of finding someone alive down there are slim," Farmer observed grimly. "But with that pocket of air inside the hull, you never know."

Lon knelt on the edge of the RHIB. "Remember, this is a trawler, so there's bound to be nets and rigging down there. Be careful."

"We will." Tyson checked his breathing apparatus.

Linc was one jump ahead. He acknowledged Lon's warning with a thumbs up before flipping backward over the edge into the water. Tyson followed his lead. Together they ducked beneath the surface to investigate the capsized boat.

As they swam down toward the wheelhouse, Linc noted there were no nets attached to the long steel arms extending from the rear of the vessel. He felt a tap on his shoulder as he kicked toward the upside-down entrance. He stopped and turned to see Tyson.

The young sailor pointed to a tennis shoe caught on a loose piece of rigging attached to a rusted pulley. Tyson freed it and tucked the lace around his weight belt. The shoe proved a woman had been aboard and had somehow escaped.

Linc swam easily through the wheelhouse doorway. It seemed strange to enter an overturned, water-logged boat. A day bed was above him on his left, and the helm and navigation desk on his right. The radio mouthpiece drifted aimlessly, still attached to the radio by a spiral cord. Cupboard doors hung open and pots, pans, cups and several cans and packets of food had floated down to the roof. Between the rudimentary galley and the helm was a stairway.

Linc swam carefully up into what seemed to be the main living quarters. Two bunks lined one wall, and a table hung from the floor, flanked by a cushioned booth-style seat.

Linc's gaze drifted up to a pair of legs in shorts. A flash of yellow captured his attention. A body. It was floating at the waterline, the head by all appearances in the air pocket.

Linc swam alongside and surfaced. He studied the Asian man wearing a bright yellow life jacket. His eyes were closed and blood still seeped from a severe knock to his head.

Linc felt for a pulse and was stunned to actually find one. He glanced down and spotted Tyson swimming into the cavity. He surfaced on the injured man's right. Linc spat his oxygen regulator so he could speak. Tyson did the same.

"Is he dead?"

"No. Listen, we don't have much time. This whole boat could go any minute. I need you to help me remove his lifejacket while keeping his head above water. Then I'll put my mask and regulator on him so he won't drown on the way out."

The hull creaked ominously.

"It'd be so much easier if he was conscious."

Linc smiled wryly. "It's more fun this way. Hold his head up."

"Got it."

With careful manoeuvring, they freed the man of his buoyant vest. The hull gave a painful groan and the floor above them tilted.

"She's going down."

Linc heard nervous tension in his comrade's tone. He forced down panic and kept his movements calm and measured. He cleared his regulator by exhaling sharply. He placed it in the unconscious sailor's mouth. Tyson held it in place while Linc then fastened the mask.

Bubbles gurgled as the air pocket decreased and the boat tilted further.

"Go!" Linc nodded toward the stairway which was steadily rising with the lift of the sinking vessel.

Tyson cleared his regulator and hastily dove for the exit. Linc took one last deep breath, and with an arm around the unconscious man, and a hand holding the mouthpiece in place, he kicked toward the stairs.

He tried to swim through the gap and realised after the first attempt that they would not fit all at once. He wasn't about to remove his hand from the regulator, or in his unconscious state, the injured man's jaw would relax and the mouthpiece would come out.

The boat tilted further and Linc's head bumped against the floor of the opening. His lungs demanded oxygen. He struggled to squeeze through. He succeeded, and then with a flipper either side of the stairway, gently pulled the man through.

He pushed off the cupboards with his flippers and kicked like mad for the wheelhouse doorway. It was now angled up and Linc could see daylight above the boat slipping away.

The vessel was headed for the ocean floor in a rush and nothing would stop her now.

He cleared the exit and narrowly missed one of the steel arms as the trawler began to spiral. Above him the hull of the RHIB appeared as a silhouette against a sun kissed surface. A second pair of hands came from seemingly nowhere and grabbed the unconscious man. Together Linc and Tyson powered toward the crimson and gold waves lapping at the boat above.

Linc's head breached first and he gasped for air.

"They've got someone!" Lon exclaimed and leant over the edge to pull the casualty from the water.

Farmer joined him and in moments the injured man was aboard the RHIB.

Tyson removed his head gear and grinned at the lieutenant. "You sure like to cut things close, sir."

Linc smiled and shrugged while catching his breath. "I never intend to. Things just seem to happen that way."

Tyson chuckled and took the hand Lon offered. The bosun hauled him into the inflatable. Linc exhaled slowly and listened to the sound of his heartbeat pounding in his ears. That had been a little too close for comfort, even for a thrill seeker like him.

~

Macca caught sight of the sleek white yacht on the horizon. He waved his arms like a madman. It drew steadily closer, although on a heading that would likely miss him by a couple hundred metres.

Spotting a lone man in an ocean, especially when not on the lookout for one, was next to impossible. Nevertheless, Macca kept waving and shouting until he was hoarse.

If he could survive last night's fierce storm and the shark that had curiously nudged him at dawn, then it was possible the skipper on that yacht might see him.

The expensive boat suddenly shifted on a direct course toward him. Macca continued to holler and wave. The time it took to pull alongside felt like an eternity. Yet when a deckhand reached down from the low platform at the stern, Macca was never more grateful.

~

Nethania let her head fall back against the bulky collar of the lifejacket keeping her afloat. She was freezing cold and absolutely exhausted. All she could see for kilometres in every direction was ocean. She supposed she could survive the cold and even the waves. What worried her was what lurked beneath the surface. As a marine biologist, she was deeply aware of the predators below.

Nethania clutched Padi's backpack to her chest and wept. Surely he and the skipper had perished in the storm. She was never more conscious of being alone than in that moment. She marvelled that the old saying really was true. One's life really did flash before one's eyes in dire circumstances.

She saw her mother's concerned face as she announced she was leaving the church, leaving the state, and quitting her steady job in the Sydney aquarium. Her father and even her grandmother had lodged their protests.

Desmond Brideson had cut straight to the heart of the issue.

"Running away won't heal the hurt, Nethania. They should never have treated you that way, but don't take it out on God."

"Of all the people who could have turned against me, I least expected it of my brothers and sisters in Christ. I don't want anything to do with them. And if God expects me to forgive them, He's got another thing coming!"

"Careful daughter, you're on dangerous ground. If

you don't forgive, then you won't be forgiven. Failing to love God's people, despite their faults, is failing to honour His commands, and therefore not loving God Himself."

"Yeah well, I'm not exactly thrilled with Him at the moment either," she admitted honestly.

Nethania recalled the betrayal and the hurt she had experienced. She had spent years gaining trust and credibility as a youth leader In her church. She firmly believed that saving intimacy for marriage was crucial for both moral and practical reasons. She had encouraged her youth group to follow her example and wait for the right life partner God had planned for them. She was never flirty. On the contrary, although she was friendly, she had endeavoured to treat every male as though they were someone else's future husband.

She had endorsed strong focus on education and career as well. At first she had been laughed at, but over time her consistency had earned her Christian, and non-Christian, friends' respect.

Then one day Nethania had gone diving with a friend from work, Aidan. The tide had washed higher up the beach than either of them had anticipated, drenching their clothes and towels. They had driven to Nethania's home not five minutes away to shower and change. Her best friend Alana had unexpectedly dropped by. Nethania had opted for the second shower, which was where she had been when Alana knocked.

Aidan had automatically gone to answer the door, albeit wearing only a towel while his clothes were in the dryer. Unbeknownst to Nethania at the time, Alana had made some wrong assumptions. She had then shared them with a loose-lipped member at church.

Nethania had been unable to fathom the cold shoulders she received, or the biting remarks. That was until the pastor himself had taken her to task. The fact they had all assumed the worst when she and Aidan were perfectly innocent, had wounded her deeply. Her reputation and strong moral stance had been ruined over night.

Anger arose as she recalled that terrible time six months ago. Her father's words rang in her ears, as steady as the waves lapping at her body.

"If you won't forgive then you won't be forgiven."

Her anger drained quickly. She was sure to die. Between the sharks, jellyfish, iricanji and dehydration, her chances for survival were slim to none. She had sins aplenty; pride, hate, bitterness and unforgiveness just to name a few. She had not kept God's command to love her neighbour as herself.

Could she forgive Alana and the church for their betrayal?

What about your betrayal of Me? You have made more than your fair share of assumptions. The foreign thought impressed itself upon her heart and mind.

Nethania swallowed hard. She had never considered pushing God aside as equivalent to what His people had done to her. Now the very idea shocked her.

"I'm so sorry!" A sob broke from her throat as the full import of what she had put Him through sank in.

"How are You able to forgive me?"

Because I love you. The words seemed to pass before her mind's eye, and behind them she sensed unconditional love beckoning.

Salty tears tracked down her cheeks onto her life vest, which were then claimed by the sea.

"Then help me love like You do so I can forgive too? I give up fighting You and running away. You can have my running shoes."

Something nudged her from below, so hard in fact that she did indeed lose her last sneaker. Nethania let out a startled scream and pulled her legs up to her chest, still clutching Padi's bag. An enormous shadow moved stealthily below. Her terrified gaze followed its progress toward the surface.

3

"Linc, you should get some time in your rack," Lieutenant Commander Joshua Donnelly suggested. "You were on the last watch and then that rescue you and Tys pulled... You must be beat."

The two men were in the passageway between the bridge and the wardroom, where Farmer and Lon had taken the injured sailor. Linc had stripped his wetsuit to the waist, but had not as yet had time to change since coming aboard.

His smile was dry. "I do feel tired, but that rescue kind of woke me up and now I can't sleep."

They passed the galley serving counter. "I don't suppose anyone got much sleep last night."

"Yeah I know." Linc grinned as he remembered the wild seas they had traversed. "Wasn't it a buzz? Like riding a roller coaster, only better with the super light show."

Joshua stopped outside the wardroom and turned to look at him in astonishment.

Linc stared right back, a little baffled. "What sir?"

The lieutenant commander smiled in amusement and shook his head. Linc puzzled over his reaction. What had he said that was so unusual?

Joshua stepped into the wardroom that had temporarily been converted into a sickbay. The fixed table, which was flanked by a long cushioned seat against the wall, was being used as a gurney.

The patient was stretched out on its now padded surface with his head on a pillow. His dark eyes were open and Farmer, the experienced medic on board, was using a small flashlight to check pupil dilation.

Joshua moved to the foot of the table. "How is he?"

Farmer completed his check and glanced at the captain. "He's got a concussion, but otherwise nothing seems to be broken."

Linc occupied the doorway, and from his position he could see that Farmer had already patched up the head wound. Joshua moved to the patient's side, his expression kind.

"What's your name?"

"Padi Ato." His eyes wearily drifted shut and he forced them open again. "You find Netania and Macca?"

Joshua and Linc exchanged concerned glances.

"I'll ask Shep to plot a search area." Linc turned to leave.

"No, I'll do it. You go clean up and get some sleep."

"Yes sir." Linc was not about to argue with the captain, although he was tempted. He wanted to see this through to the end. As he was leaving, he heard the lieutenant commander address the injured man.

"Mr. Ato, I need you to tell me what happened in detail."

~

Macca accepted the hot cup of coffee and revelled in its robust flavour. A gentleman in beige dress trousers, impeccably shined shoes and a loose cream shirt leaned casually against the salon doorway. He smiled and carefully assessed his guest.

"Got caught in the storm?"

"Sure did. My boat went over an' I managed to get out. I was swept away before I could find out what happened to my passengers. Hope the poor blighters got out too." He glanced around at his surroundings and finally took note of the opulence of the large salon.

Windows ran the full length of the room on each side. Long cushioned lounge suites in red formed a disjointed U shape, with four small metallic coffee tables bolted to the polished wood floor spaced between each section.

A large LCD screen television occupied the far wall, and on either side were passageways, presumably to the galley and stairways leading above to the helm, and below to the staterooms.

The gentleman crossed the short distance. "My name is Finn Cruikshank."

"Macca. Reckon you could notify the coastguard? They might be able to find my boat and my passengers." He met the yacht owner's gaze and thought he read a moment's hesitation.

A friendly smile appeared. "Of course."

No, Macca must have imagined it. The man couldn't be nicer.

"Where can we drop you?"

"Where you headed? Don't wanna put you out of your way."

"It's no trouble," the middle-aged man assured graciously.

"Cairns'll do."

Finn nodded and his smile was relaxed. "I shall speak with my skipper."

With that he left. Macca supposed he was meant to stay put, but he wanted to talk to the skipper himself. He would be able to give him the last known coordinates for The Queen Maree.

He gulped the last few mouthfuls of coffee and sat the empty mug on the nearest metallic cocktail table. He saw none of the crew in the vicinity and decided he would find his own way to the helm.

He wandered past the TV mounted on the wall, down a short passage on his right and noted a spiral staircase. He heard male voices drifting downward and recognised Finn's. The helm had to be up those stairs. He started up the carpet covered steps and froze halfway as what was being said fully registered.

"It's a bad idea Finn. I just received a radio call from The HMAS Hartfield asking if we'd picked up anyone adrift in the storm."

"What did you say?"

"I said no of course. The last thing we want is the

navy sniffing around."

"Fair enough, Gareth. All the same, it won't hurt to drop the man off at the nearest port."

"And if he finds what's hidden below?"

"Then we'll take care of him." Finn's tone was decidedly sinister.

Macca swallowed hard. What were they hiding below deck? Could they really be contemplating killing him? He stealthily crept back down the stairs and returned to the salon. Only then did he realise he had left a water trail on the polished floor boards.

4

The huge aquatic mammal surfaced only metres from Nethania and released a burst of vapour from its blow hole. She exhaled in relief, recognising the distinctive lines of a humpback whale. It's mother surfaced not twenty metres beyond it.

The juvenile was the size of an elephant, and its mother at least two to three times that. The young humpback curiously eyed Nethania before following after its mother.

The marine biologist in her puzzled for a moment. It was calving season, and humpbacks traditionally nursed their young in warmer coastal waters not far from the shore to protect them from predators.

Why was this mother so far from the coast? Or was she? Hope burgeoned. Nethania's gaze followed the direction the whales were taking. A sob of pure relief broke from her throat. On the horizon, rising from the midst of the ocean, was a group of lush green islands.

"Thank You God!"

Nethania began paddling toward them.

~

Lieutenant Commander Donnelly sighed and wearily rubbed his face. He stared out at a dark ocean under a velvet black sky glittering with sparkling diamonds from his place in the captain's chair. Conditions couldn't be better. All the same, their day long search had been fruitless. He silently prayed for a breakthrough.

The chances of survival in these waters for this length of time were slim. There were too many adverse factors in play.

"Captain, we have a contact."

It didn't matter that Joshua was only a lieutenant commander. The sailor in charge of the boat was always referred to as captain.

"Read its position Shep."

The navigator was sitting adjacent from him in front of the high definition navigational radar.

"Seventeen degrees latitude, one hundred and forty-nine degrees longitude."

Joshua's interest peaked. "Size?"

"Likely a small fishing vessel or a pleasure craft."

Joshua glanced over his shoulder at the communications desk. "Woody, make radio contact."

Leading Seaman Underwood obeyed. "Vessel seventeen degrees latitude, one hundred and forty-nine degrees longitude, bearing northeast, this is The HMAS Hartfield. Do you copy?"

The VHF produced only static. Woody repeated his call and waited. He looked ready to try again when a distinctly Australian accent came over the radio.

"Yeah HMAS Hartfield, this is The Charlene. What can we do for ya?"

Woody glanced at the captain and handed over the receiver.

"This is the captain speaking. Have you happened to come across an older man or a young woman adrift?"

Joshua knew it was a long shot. Aside from the low light optical equipment, there was not much else they could do at night to find the missing skipper and marine biologist. A P3 Orion might prove useful in the morning, and with the coastguard out looking too, they might stand a chance.

"They got the navy out searchin'?" An amazed chuckle followed the comment. "Of all the luck! Yeah, we 'ave. Picked up a rough bloke named Macca in an inflatable just on dusk. He reckoned the yacht that picked 'im up today was carryin' dodgy cargo. He swears black an' blue the skipper had it in for 'im. Crazy bloke stole a raft an' disappeared over the edge. We got 'im in a rack below sleepin' it off."

Joshua's brows rose sharply and he exchanged glances with Woody. To his navigator he said, "How long will it take us to rendezvous?"

"An hour tops."

"Get us there." While Joshua returned his attention to the skipper on the other end of the radio and pressed the transmission button, his navigator gave a new heading for the helmsman. "Can you drop anchor for an hour? We're on our way to collect the man."

"Can do. See you soon."

"Hartfield over." Joshua passed the receiver to Woody and returned to his chair. All the while he silently gave God thanks.

Shep met his gaze and grinned. "Two survivors recovered. Only one to go."

A tangible sense of relief and hope buzzed throughout the bridge, and with it a renewed sense of purpose.

~

Nethania huddled under a layer of palm fronds and shivered. Waves curled onto the sand before her in a steady rhythm. At her back, dense forest reached toward a glittering night sky. Their leaves rustled gently in a soft breeze.

Nature's peaceful lullaby failed to reassure her. She had never been more exhausted in her life. However, her racing mind refused sleep. Were Macca and Padi alive? Had Macca's mayday been successful? How long would it be before people noticed they were missing? Would the coastguard initiate a search, or would they be given up for dead?

Nethania's heart plummeted with that last thought. Her mother and father might very well be informed soon that their daughter had died at sea. What pained her most, was that they were unaware she had made her peace with God. Would they believe her lost forever?

Tears flooded her tired eyes and she wept.

~

"How is he, Farmer?"

Joshua carefully studied The Hartfield's medic for signs of stress or fatigue. It was the early hours of the morning and Farmer was reporting to him on the bridge.

They had come alongside The Charlene, a rough looking fishing vessel, half an hour ago. Lon had taken care of the transfer and conferred with its crew. The ordeal the skipper of The Queen Maree had been through was still somewhat of a mystery.

"He's still dehydrated and his blood pressure is slightly elevated. Otherwise he's in good health."

Joshua rubbed his stiff neck and offered a smile. "That's good news, all things considered. Did he say anything about the woman?"

Farmer shook his head no. "He was swept away by another wave before she surfaced. Tyso found her shoe caught in the rigging, so she must have made it out."

"Does Macca know if she had a life vest on?"

"Yes, she did."

"Alright, we'll extend the search area. Go get some sleep."

The medic nodded and descended from the bridge.

Joshua turned to the navigator, who was already studying a nautical chart beneath a glass top on a fixed table. It was against the waist high partition beside the stairs.

"What do you think?"

Shep's brow furrowed. "I allowed for winds and currents, but in the dark we could sail right past her and never know. Spotlights can only shine so far."

"We'll have daylight soon. Extend the area to account for the added day she's been in the drink."

"Will do." Shep used a whiteboard marker and ruler on the glass top to widen the search zone.

"In the meantime, let's check out this yacht Macca believes is suspicious."

5

Cold water rushed over Nethania and roused her abruptly from a fitful sleep. She gasped and bolted upright. The rising tide had reached the top of the beach where she had spent the night. She frowned and wiped sand from her cheek. Where was the life jacket? She had been using it as a pillow.

Another wave rushed up the beach and drenched her to the waist. The last vestiges of sleep evaporated as she exclaimed and leapt to her feet. The last of her frond blanket washed down into the ocean, and she understood what had become of her vest. She had to have rolled over in her sleep in the early hours of morning and the tide must have claimed it.

Nethania stumbled from the sand into the tree line and rubbed chilled arms. The warm tropical sun would no doubt dry her soaked clothing in record time. All the same, she could have done without the rude awakening.

She glanced around in disorientation. Her gaze came to rest upon Padi's backpack. Nethania was grateful she'd had the presence of mind to dump it above the sand just inside the trees. Her stomach rumbled. She decided it was time to see what Padi had inside his bag that might prove useful in her quest for food.

~

Linc stepped onto the thirty-seven metre white yacht followed by the bosun. Woody, Coz, Tyso, and Tommo the ship's chef, were next. Farmer remained at the wheel in the RHIB. As was customary, each member of the boarding party was armed with pistols in a holster strapped to their right leg, and wearing dark blue Kevlar plated vests. However, this time as they boarded, their manner was relaxed. This was an Australian vessel in Australian waters and they needed to tread carefully.

A middle-aged gentleman with dark hair receding around his wide forehead approached the boarding party with an easygoing smile.

"Welcome aboard. I'm Finn Cruickshank. What can I do for you?"

Linc shook the hand he offered and smiled politely. "Lieutenant Hobbs, Executive Officer of the HMAS Hartfield." He allowed his appreciative gaze to wander over the impressive vessel. "This is a nice boat you've got. A Majesty 121 motor yacht, right?"

Finn's head tilted in surprise. "You know your boats, although I guess that's to be expected of a navy man."

Linc grinned. "Enough to appreciate two MTU 16V M93 2000 hp engines and to know I'll never be able to afford them on navy wages."

Finn laughed good-naturedly and indicated for his

unexpected guests to enter the main salon. "Come on in."

Linc and Lon exchanged glances. Experience had taught them both never to trust anyone upon a first meeting, no matter how congenial.

"Did the captain explain the reason for our boarding when he contacted you by radio minutes ago?" Linc followed the man into the impressive main entertainment area.

Rich red suede lounge suites formed a U shape and were bolted onto highly polished floorboards. The junior sailors followed the bosun and XO, unable to hide their awe over the luxury cruiser. Their wide eyes swept the room in admiration. Tommo nudged Coz and nodded toward the opulent furniture and large LCD TV mounted in the far wall.

"You gotta be mad to jump off a boat like this," Linc heard him whisper.

Coz's awed gaze swept the room one more time. "Yeah."

Linc cast them both a warning glance to keep quiet and stay on task.

"No, he didn't. I must say that I *am* curious," Finn answered and dropped onto one of the couches. He gestured for his guests to have a seat opposite him.

Linc smiled and politely declined with a wave of his hand and a slight shake of his head. "Sorry, but we have orders to search your vessel. A man you rescued named Macca, was concerned you were carrying suspicious cargo. As you can understand, we're required by law to check any such accusations out." Linc kept his tone and manner pragmatic.

Finn nodded and stood. "I wondered why he jumped ship. He had been gone an hour before we noticed. We reversed course and searched while we had daylight, but couldn't find him."

"Did you inform the coastguard?" Lon queried.

"Of course." Finn remained calm and his voice reasonable. "He was an odd one. He probably took in a little too much sun and sea water."

"It's possible," Lon agreed to keep the atmosphere friendly.

Having talked in depth with the skipper of The Queen Maree that morning, Linc doubted that was the case. The man was rough around the edges personality wise, but he was no fool.

"I would like all of your crew on the main deck please," Linc requested.

"Sure, I'll have Gareth put it over the intercom." Finn started toward the stairs behind the partition at the end of the room.

"I'll do that." Linc stopped him with a smile and strode toward the wheelhouse. He glanced over his shoulder at his men. "Coz and Tommo, stay here with the crew. Tyso and Lon, begin searching the rooms below. Start with the cargo hold. I'll head to the wheelhouse and then join you."

He glanced at the owner of the yacht. "Mr. Cruickshank, would you kindly wait with my men on the deck?"

"It's my pleasure to accommodate you," Finn answered graciously.

~

"There's nothing here, sir," Linc informed the captain via radio transmission, as he stood in the salon after an extensive search of the vessel.

"Roger that," Joshua replied, his voice coming clear through Linc's headset. "I've informed Navcom of Macca's allegations. It's up to the feds now. Time you boys wrapped it up. We've had a contact. It's Ollie from The Dream Catcher. He was out on a tour that happened to be in the search area. He found a lifejacket adrift with the words 'Queen Maree' printed on the back."

"The missing marine biologist?"

"Seems she hasn't survived. Navcom has called off the search."

Linc's heart sank. "Is there a body?" He had truly believed they would find her.

"Not likely, not with the sharks."

"Copy that. Over." Linc strode to the stern where the crew and his men were waiting. "Alright boys, it's time we let these good folks head on their way." He made eye contact with Finn. "Sorry about the inconvenience."

He extended his hand and the wealthy businessman shook it.

"Not a hassle. I understand. I hope next time we

bump into you it will be under better circumstances." Finn smiled and waved a friendly farewell as the navy sailors climbed over the edge into the waiting RHIB.

As Farmer sped toward the patrol boat waiting sixty metres away, Lon glanced at the executive officer.

"You know he was lying."

Linc sighed. "Yep."

"Then why be nice to him?" Coz piped up from the seat in front of the helm.

Linc was standing beside Farmer, holding onto a handrail. "You catch more flies with honey than vinegar." He smiled sagely at the boatswain's mate.

Coz grinned.

6

Nethania sat the sturdy stick aside on a bed of leaves. A medium sized fish was still impaled on Padi's knife tied to the end.

"At least I'm not useless."

She dropped down onto the forest floor beside Padi's backpack, feeling proud of her catch. Now all she needed was matches so she could make a fire and roast her meal. She wasn't partial to sushi.

Nethania dumped the contents of the bag for the second time that day. Everything inside had been sopping wet, however the warm tropical sun had quickly dried it out. She surveyed the odd assortment and was thrilled to find a cigarette lighter. Padi did not smoke. She smiled.

"He's just a big Boy Scout." Her smile faded. Had he gotten out? "Please Father in heaven, let him be alive?"

Weighty thoughts gave way to a feeling of wonderment. Speaking to God again was as natural as breathing. She marvelled that she had been able to pick up where she had left off. She had once been so close to Him that He had been to her a true father, so much so she used to call Him Papa. The distance of their time apart dropped away and she began to think of

Him that way again. Regret chased in on the heels of wonder. She was sorry to have squandered the last six months.

"Papa, I'm ashamed to think what I've done to You. Please forgive me?"

Peace washed over her gently like the rising tide.

"Now Papa, to redeem the time I've lost..."

She resolutely arose and set about building a camp fire on the beach. It would serve two purposes. The first being to cook her food. The second to signal passing ships.

~

Joshua saluted the Australian flag flying on The Hartfield before he strode across the gangway onto the dock. All non-essential crew had already disembarked. They were all on call and could be crash sailed at a moment's notice. He had finally tied up the mountain of paperwork on his desk and completed debriefing his superiors. Padi and Macca had been safely delivered to port and were met by police, who would take statements.

Joshua stopped at the bottom of the gangway and smiled. Standing several metres away was his eight month pregnant wife and his two-year-old daughter. Joey Donnelly's half moon eyes sparkled with delight and a light breeze tussled loose strands of long ebony hair. One and a half children later, and he still thought her as beautiful as the day he had married her.

"Daddy!" With an enormous grin, Faith ran toward him with outstretched arms.

Joshua laughed and swept her up for a cuddle and a kiss. The little girl was a miniature clone of her mother with her distinct Asian features and tanned skin. However, her eyes were a vivid blue, just like her father.

"How's my gorgeous girl? Have you been taking care of your mum?"

Faith's smile was huge as she nodded.

"Good." Joshua closed the distance between he and his wife. With Faith still on one arm, he pulled Joey close for a greeting kiss. "I've missed you two!"

"Well, we've got you to ourselves for the better part of three days," Joey consoled in a broad Australian accent.

Joshua was momentarily distracted when he spotted his executive officer not five metres further down the dock looking concerned. He appeared to be scrolling through messages on his cell phone.

"Everything alright?"

Linc glanced up after he dialled a number. "I hope so."

The call must have gone through, for his whole attention turned to the person on the other end of the line. Not wanting to eavesdrop, Joshua chose to discreetly steer his family toward their car.

Joey's gaze lingered on their mutual friend as they passed by. "He does look rather upset. Perhaps we should wait a few minutes?"

Joshua glanced over his shoulder and then at their car not far away. "He's a big boy. If he needs help, he knows where we live."

Joey took his logic on board and visibly relaxed. Joshua grinned at her. It was good to be home, even if only for a few days.

~

Linc listened to several urgent messages from the hospital and then dialled them directly. He wondered who he knew around town that could possibly be ill. His family lived in Western Australia and had declared years ago that they wanted nothing to do with their black sheep son. The fact he had joined the navy shortly after he left home at nineteen and turned his life around, meant little to his dogmatic and inflexible parents.

He still recalled the day his father had dejectedly commented that Linc was his greatest disappointment. The only member of his family who seemed able to forget his wild youth was his sister Jaclyn.

Linc shook his mind free of those dark days as he listened to the dial tone in his ear. Finally a receptionist picked up.

"Cairns Hospital. This is Linda speaking. How may I help you?"

"Yeah hi Linda. I'm Lincoln Hobbs. I've been at sea on patrol. I've just now received a bunch of messages from the hospital. Can you tell me what's going on?"

There was a pause. "Ah yes, I've got a note here on my desk. It says that it's urgent you come in to neonatal."

Linc frowned. "Neonatal? Why?"

"I'm not sure. I'm just to tell you if you call that it's urgent."

He exhaled slowly and puzzled over the request. "Alright. I'll come straight over."

"Thank you Mr. Hobbs. I'll inform the staff you've been in touch and are on your way."

Linc disconnected the line and stared at the phone in his hand. With an uneasy cloud brooding over his heart, he picked up the bag at his feet and sought his car.

~

Nethania's stomach was finally satisfied and she was able to turn her attention to other items from Padi's pack. The fire crackled comfortingly beside her, and with her legs stretched out, she emptied the bag.

Item by item, she began to examine its contents. Goggles, snorkel, wallet, a change of clothes, a waterlogged iPhone, a square sealed tin, and a small leather toiletries bag. Nethania studied each object and became intensely curious over the tin. She had seen him on occasion in his bunk with it open. He had hastily packed it away each time upon her entrance.

She took the tin in her hands and worked the tight-ly sealed lid off. She stared in bewilderment at the strange compilation of documents. There was a map of the Great Barrier Reef with a red X over a spot not far from a small grouping of islands. She recognised the location. It was one of the areas they had intended to survey over the next few weeks. In fact, if her estima-tion was correct, she was on one of those islands now. She had seen Macca aim his trawler for them during the storm.

Putting the map aside, she lifted out a black and white photograph of two Japanese sailors, bare-chest-ed and in shorts. They were aboard what appeared to be a World War Two navy ship. At their feet on the deck was a chest, partially rotted away in places. It's lid was open and inside were gold and jewels. Behind the men were three chests just like it.

Nethania was stunned. Whoever these men were, they had obviously found sunken treasure. She placed the photograph with the map and took out the remain-ing documents. There were three letters all written in Japanese, and each yellowed with age.

Finally, there was a short historical article in English. She briefly scanned it. The clipping told of a Dutch explorer by the name of Salomon Chan who had set out to find the Great South Land in 1759. He had sailed from the Dutch East Indies, now known as Indonesia, in his ship The Hildegard, and had never been heard from since. The article outlined other explorers who had travelled along the coasts of Australia prior to captain

James Cook's voyage and the subsequent settlement of the southern continent by the British.

Nethania was baffled. How were all of the documents related? Why were they of interest to Padi? She placed them back in the tin. As she did, she noticed writing in English on the back of the photograph. It said simply: Yadi Kado, Mahito Aiji, 1942.

Nethania's brows drew together suspiciously. The name Kado was familiar. Padi had been the one to find a wealthy benefactor to finance their research voyage. He had told her he'd known the man since childhood. What was his name again? She wracked her brain until finally it came.

Dake. His name was Dake Kado. Was he somehow related to Yadi in the photograph, and if so, why had he really financed their research?

Padi had explained their benefactor only wanted some coral and tropical fish that were native to Australian waters in exchange. Now she was beginning to doubt her colleague. Did he have a hidden agenda?

7

"Please have a seat Mr. Hobbs."

The Indian doctor was a young looking man, possibly in his early thirties. His kind brown eyes were as dark as his chocolate toned skin.

Linc sat in the small waiting area just outside the neonatal ward at the local hospital. Staff and visitors alike bustled past in a steady procession, but he no longer noticed. The gravity in the doctor's expression was beginning to trigger alarm bells.

"What's going on?"

"Do you know a Miss Tessa Channing?"

Linc's heart froze in his chest. Had something happened to his ex-girlfriend? "We dated for a year. Five months ago she broke it off and skipped town. I haven't heard from her since."

The doctor's eyes filled with compassion. "I am sorry, Mr. Hobbs. She has passed away."

Linc sprang from his seat. "What? That's not possible!"

"There were complications during her labour and we were unable to save her."

The doctor's words drummed into his awareness. "Labour? She was pregnant?"

The physician studied him quizzically. "She never told

you she was carrying your child?"

Linc's sane, stable world rocked on its axis.

My child?

He sank onto a chair and struggled to comprehend those two small words. She had been expecting? Linc rested his elbows on his knees and cradled his head in his hands.

"Oh Tess, why did you leave?" He lamented in a whisper.

She had needed him and he had loved her. If only she had told him! Tears clouded his vision.

Dead.

"I can see this is a great shock, Mr. Hobbs, but you need to think about your daughter."

Linc's eyes closed and tears spilled over.

Daughter?

He was still reeling over Tessa's death and the fact she had been expecting. He wiped his face free of moisture with the back of a sun bronzed hand and drew a steady breath. "What complications?"

"Severe preeclampsia."

Linc must have looked as confused as he felt.

"High blood pressure. Her kidneys failed. We were managing that when she had a stroke."

"A stroke?" Utter bewilderment laced his emotion-choked voice and he stared at his hands which were beginning to tremble. "She was only young."

"It was because of her extremely high blood pressure. Mr. Hobbs, I know this is a lot to take in at one time, but your girlfriend has been deceased for a week and we need to know what to do with baby Yasmin."

Linc sniffed and looked up at the physician. "She named her?"

"Yes. She listed you as next of kin and gave us your name and number. She said she had flown to Cairns to be with you. We think the flight may have been a contributing factor in the complications she suffered."

Linc's heart squeezed painfully. She had come home only to die like this? "Did she give you my number because she knew she was dying?"

"No, although she understood her condition was serious. We were thinking only of family members who might be able to offer her and the baby support."

Linc stared blankly across the hallway. "She had no family. She was shuffled from one foster home to the next as a kid after her grandmother died."

Silence lingered, and so did the question of the baby's future.

"Yasmin is healthy and ready to go home," the doctor ventured carefully. "If you cannot raise her, human services will find a placement for the child."

Something inside Linc rebelled and he felt like a knife had been plunged into his chest. Tessa would hate for her child to grow up in the welfare system as she had. The possibility of an adoption was high, but still...

Linc heard words coming from his mouth as though someone else was speaking them. "No, I'll take her."

"Good." The doctor nodded decisively. "Wait here a moment and I will get a nurse who will show you to your daughter. You will have paper work to complete as well before you can leave with her."

Numbness started to creep over Linc. His daughter.

In the space of five minutes he had gone from the carefree life of a bachelor, to a father. Aside from feeling lost and overwhelmed by grief, fear began to tug at his heart. How was he supposed to care for an infant when he was at sea up to three weeks at a time? He shoved those thoughts aside. First he would meet his child.

8

Nethania powered up a hill a couple of hundred metres inland, weaving between tall broad-leafed evergreens and stepping over protruding roots. The forest floor was literally a carpet of decaying wood and leaves, all decomposing at a faster rate. This was due to the inability of the sun to fully penetrate the maze of thick leaves and branches in the canopy above. In patches where it was able to break through, ferns, shrubs, small trees and woody vines proliferated.

She reached the top and pushed through a tangle of plants with large leaves attempting to catch what little sunlight was available. The sound of trickling water reached her ears and she walked faster. She ducked beneath a snaking vine that was climbing around a stout tree trunk, and then spotted it.

A pool of crystal clear water, roughly two metres in diameter, trickled over surrounding rocks, forming a stream that wove between ancient evergreens. The water in the pool bubbled happily and a grin found Nethania's lips.

A freshwater spring!

"The Lord is my shepherd, I shall not want," she quoted softly and knelt to drink.

When her thirst had abated, she sat beside the pool

and let her eyes roam her surroundings. She etched this place into her memory. If she was not rescued soon, she would need to visit this spring often.

Worry nagged at her, and with it the pain of betrayal. The past reared its head and joined her present distress. She voiced her thoughts in prayer, speaking as though God was sitting right beside her, and in truth she believed He was even closer than that.

"First it's my best friend and then the church family who make wrong assumptions and then turn on me, and now I discover Padi hasn't been honest. I feel like I've been completely let down and used. I have to admit, God, that I have no trust left."

She waited in the silence that followed and was not at all surprised by the gentle voice that arose within her. The words that nudged her consciousness were not her own, and from years of learning to listen to that voice, she recognised its source.

You may trust Me whole heartedly. Unlike mankind, I will never let you down. I speak only the truth. My motive is pure love and righteousness. I am the one who heals you. Give me forty days on this island that I may work to this end?

Nethania's brows quirked in surprise. "You want me to stay on this island forty more days? How on earth will I survive, Papa?"

I will provide for you. Will you trust Me?

Nethania thought the request over for several uncomfortable minutes. There were so many loose ends in her life that needed tying up; her friends, her family,

Padi and his secret documents, and finally her work. She simply did not have time to waste on this island!

You have run from Me, ignored Me and shoved me aside for the past six months. Is forty days really too much to ask?

The astonishing challenge left her momentarily speechless and feeling a good deal of shame. After a lengthy thoughtful silence, she was finally able to offer a heartfelt answer.

"I'm sorry, Papa. You may have all the time You want. I am Yours."

A strange sense of delight tickled her awareness, but the emotion was not hers. She frowned and could not resist a curious smile toward the heavens. Just what was God up to? What did He have planned that brought Him such joy?

~

The tiniest hand Linc had ever seen wrapped around his index finger with amazing strength. A love he had never known he was capable of surged through him powerfully as he held the infant girl in his arms for the first time. Tears unexpectedly gathered in his green eyes. She was simply beautiful.

Her dark lashes were little fans against creamy white cheeks and her delicate mouth was the shape of an archer's bow. Light coloured hair covered her small head in a layer of fuzz. Linc gently stroked it and was amazed by its softness.

He knew in that moment he could never give her up. His previous decision to keep her had been out of love and loyalty to Tessa. Now as he held their child in his arms, his choice was cemented by love for the little girl, who even at this early stage resembled her mother. He had no idea how to make it work, but he was determined that he would.

"I'll show you how to bath and change her now if you'd like," the nurse gently offered.

Linc glanced to his right in surprise, having forgotten she was at his side. He quickly blinked back tears before nodding assent. The woman smiled to herself as she began preparations to bath the child.

She spent the next half hour patiently teaching him the basics of how to care for her. Linc realised it was a crash course and would not be enough, but for now it would have to do. The demands on the limited staff were many and he knew she simply did not have more time to offer.

~

"Jaclyn, I don't really know what to say, just that I'm in way over my head and I really need help. Call me when you can. Linc."

He disconnected the line after leaving the message on his sister's home phone and stared at the infant sleeping on the table in the portable capsule he had just bought. He supposed she would need a crib and a whole lot of other baby paraphernalia.

He rubbed his face wearily. He was supposed to sail in three days. Who would care for her then? He considered calling his parents and quickly dismissed that idea. His predicament would only confirm their negative view regarding their son.

Doubt crashed over him like a breaker and suddenly he was no longer sure of himself. Maybe they were right?

A sheet of white on the floor beside the table caught his eye. He frowned and picked it up. He recognised the handwriting and grief burrowed its knife deep in his chest. Tessa had been here? She must have kept her key. How had her note ended up on the floor? He remembered the gust of wind that had accompanied his entrance to the small cottage on the beachfront and thought he could make a pretty good guess.

Linc scanned the missive and then read it again, finding both a small measure of comfort and a boat load of regret.

'Linc, I'm sorry I left the way I did five months ago. When you proposed I guess I flipped out. You know my story. I never had a great experience of what a family should be and the examples of marriage I saw were not that good either. I was afraid. I'm hoping you'll be able to forgive me and really hoping you'll take me back. I know, always the dreamer.

I haven't been able to reach you on your phone so

HIDDEN

I'm guessing you're way out at sea. I couldn't remember your e-mail address, which is why I dropped by to leave you this note. Call me on the number below when you get in. We need to talk.

Love, Tess.'

If only he had been here! He would have received her in a heartbeat. This time Linc allowed his emotions full expression. Gut wrenching sobs racked his body and broken tears coursed down his cheeks.

If only...

9

Ollie and Dayne pulled the last body from the water onto their charter boat and laid it beside the other four. One child, a teenager, a middle-aged couple, presumably their parents, and an old woman who was possibly their grandmother.

The two women wore traditional long Middle Eastern tunics and head coverings. Having spent a lot of years in the navy, Ollie quickly deducted their origin.

"Refugees?" Dayne guessed in a subdued voice.

Ollie nodded. "Most likely from Iraq or Iran. Although how they ended up out here in only a raft is beyond me."

The two fishermen surveyed the family with a sense of heaviness. How had they died? There were no marks on their bodies and they looked as though they had simply gone to sleep. Dehydration? It was more than likely out in the middle of the ocean.

Movement behind Ollie drew his attention to the young couple they had been about to take diving on the barrier reef. Both were ashen and appeared to be visibly shaken. Ollie didn't feel much better, and by the look of Dayne, he didn't either.

"I'll go call it in. Hopefully a navy patrol or the coast guard will be in the area." Ollie's eyes shifted to the makeshift raft now tied to the back of the boat.

Dayne covered the family with a tarpaulin. "I'm beginning to think we're bad luck."

Ollie smiled grimly at his first mate's black humour and strode to the radio in the wheelhouse.

~

"Tell daddy what you think we should call the new baby," Joey prompted her daughter.

The little girl was tucked beneath her covers and Joshua was sitting on the edge of the bed, having just finished reading her a picture storybook. Joey was standing to the side, enjoying the interchange between father and child.

Joshua exchanged smiles with his wife and turned his attention to the delightful two-year-old. Her vivid blue eyes looked up at him seriously.

"Shrek."

Joey's dark eyes lit with amusement. "And if it's a girl?"

"Pwincess Fiona."

Joshua could not hold his laughter. Joey chuckled and the little girl grinned at them both.

"We talk to Desus now?" Faith asked when her father's mirth subsided.

Joshua smiled warmly at the adorable child. "Yes."

They prayed together as a family and said goodnight. Joshua turned off the bedside lamp and followed his wife to the living room. They had just sat down when the door bell rang. Joey looked at him sideways.

"There's no way I'm getting up off this couch if I don't have to." She indicated her round belly.

Joshua smiled in amusement and rose to see who had come to visit. Even before he reached the entrance, he could hear a baby squalling. He frowned in puzzlement and opened the door. Standing on the front porch was Linc with a screaming infant in his arms. Joshua's brows shot up.

The unusual sight of his adventurous executive officer with a child brought a smile of amusement. "Have you got babysitting duties, Linc?"

"You could say that."

Joshua noted the lack of humour in his friend's expression and sobered. He held the door wide for him to enter. Joey must have heard the baby crying. She met the men in the front hallway.

She spotted the howling infant, obviously read distress in Linc's eyes, and immediately assessed the situation, as Joshua knew she would. She came forward and took the child, easing the moment with a delighted smile.

"What a gorgeous baby!" She spoke to the child in a voice that was usually able to coax forth smiles. "Yes you are. You are gorgeous!"

She tickled the baby's stomach and the crying stopped. She glanced up at Linc and offered a welcoming greeting. "I'm glad you dropped by. You've been on my mind all afternoon. Come on in." With that she turned and strode to the living room, fully expecting to be followed.

At first Linc looked stunned, and then he threw his hands in the air. "How did she do that? Yasmin's been screaming for an hour now."

Joshua chuckled and clapped his friend on the back. "It's a gift. Can I offer you coffee?"

"A cold beer would be better."

Joshua shrugged apologetically. "Sorry mate, we don't drink. How about a coke?"

"That'll do." Linc rubbed the back of his neck and appeared somewhat uncomfortable.

"What's taking you boys so long?" Joey's voice floated through to the hallway.

Joshua watched anxiety chase across the younger man's face and followed his wife's example of playing it cool. "You better do what she says. I've discovered it's easier that way."

Linc's lips quirked in a brief smile. He wandered into the living room and dropped onto the couch, a place he had spent many an evening watching football games with his boss, Wilko, Lon and a few other friends of the family. Joshua headed to the kitchen to fetch a can of coke for their guest.

~

Linc watched Joey pat Yasmin's back and wondered what she was doing. Whatever it was, it had the desired effect. The baby had stopped crying and was even beginning to look a little sleepy.

"I think she's just got a bit of wind."

As if to justify Joey, the infant let out a belch. Linc snorted in amusement.

"I can't believe something so small can be so gross."

Joey seemed to see right through his easygoing exterior. "What's going on, Linc? You're trying to hide it, but I can tell you've got the weight of the world on your shoulders."

Linc studied her quietly and then let his head fall back against the couch wearily. "Tess came back while I was at sea."

Joey's eyes lit with understanding. It was no secret that Linc had mourned her abrupt departure for months.

"Where is she now?"

Tears welled beneath Linc's closed lids. He lifted his head and blinked them away. "She died in childbirth a week ago. I didn't even know she was expecting."

Joey's eyes clouded with pain. Linc knew she and Joshua did not agree with his and Tessa's decision to live together before marriage. However, he was grateful they had never judged them and had always shown they cared.

Joshua entered in time to hear this revelation. He passed Linc the cold can and sat on the other end of the couch to listen. Linc accepted it with a thankful glance.

"I found a note at my place. She apologised for leaving the way she did and even asked if I would take her back. She tried to call my mobile while I was at sea. It wasn't until we docked that I checked my messages and found the hospital had been trying to get in contact all week. Apparently she had pre-something or other and the plane ride she took to get here didn't help."

"Preeclampsia?" Joey guessed, her gaze compassionate.

Linc nodded. "That sounds like it. The doctor said she died of a stroke due to high blood pressure." He shook his head in bewilderment. "I always hoped she would come back. I just never thought it would end like this."

He drew a shuddering breath and swallowed hard in an attempt to avoid breaking down.

"I'm sorry, Linc." Joshua's expression was one of grief and compassion.

The grieving thirty-one-year-old blinked back more tears. He raised his hands helplessly, unopened coke and all. "I don't know what to do. We sail in three days and I've got no one to look after her. There is no way I'm giving her up, so don't even think of suggesting it."

"I would never do that. I don't know if I ever told you, Linc, but my first wife died in a car accident, taking our unborn son with her. I'm grateful you haven't lost Yasmin too."

Linc looked at his commanding officer with renewed appreciation and respect. "What should I do?"

"Have you got any family who might be able to

help?"

Linc smiled, only this time without humour. "My parents think of me as the family's black sheep and haven't talked to me since I was nineteen. This will only confirm everything they believe about me to date."

Joey looked aghast. "Surely not!"

"They're self-righteous and anyone else who doesn't think like they do is destined for hell." Linc's tone was acidic. He immediately felt guilty and awkward. "Sorry. I didn't mean that against you. I know you're religious and all. I just-"

"Relax," Joey calmly interrupted. Yasmin was now cradled in her arms, fast asleep. "Sin is sin Linc, and I won't gloss over it or say that it's okay. By the same token, everyone sins and we're in no position to judge you. We all need mercy. That's the beauty of the love and grace of God."

With a meaningful glance toward her husband, she ploughed ahead. "Until you figure out what to do, Yasmin can stay with us while you're at sea."

Joshua opened his mouth to protest. Joey calmly held his gaze.

"Don't you dare go there, Josh!"

He frowned. "Go where?"

She gave him an amused smile. "You were about to argue that because I get tired it's a bad idea. Well I've got something to say to you."

Linc listened in amazement to the small woman in the armchair opposite them as she put his commanding officer back in his place. He could not resist a smile.

"What kind of children of God would we be if we sent Linc away tonight and prayed for him, but did nothing to help in his time of need? I won't do it, Josh, and don't you ask me to! Linc needs someone to look after Yasmin until he works out his situation, and what do you know," her tone lightened, "our house is perfectly set up for a new baby. And don't you give me that look!" She wagged a finger at him.

Joshua must have found it very difficult to maintain the frown he had been wearing. He clearly thought she was just too cute when she was mad. At least Linc thought so.

"I take your point. But soon enough you're going to have a newborn of your own to deal with and you'll be exhausted before it even comes."

"Rubbish." Joey brushed this aside. "When I get tired I'll call my parents. They'll come and stay a few days like they usually do, and you know my mother loves to dote on Faith. She'll be beside herself when she meets this little one."

Joey glanced down at the infant in her arms with a warm glow in her dark eyes. "Don't worry, us girls will be just fine."

Joshua's gaze was warm as well, only his was trained upon his wife. Linc hated asking for help, yet was desperate enough right now to accept it gratefully.

Joey stared at him squarely. "So, Linc, is it a deal?"

"You're one special lady, Joey Donnelly," he replied softly, gratitude in his green eyes.

Joey grinned. "And don't you be forgetting it."

Some of the tightness in his chest loosened and Linc smiled. For the first time that day he had hope that everything might eventually work out.

10

Nethania stood upon an outcropping of rocks that extended ten or so metres from the southern tip of the island. Behind her the sandy shore stretched to the east and west for several kilometres. Before her she saw only ocean and brilliant blue sky. Crystal clear water lapped against the rocks at her feet in a gentle never ending cycle.

The paradise around her was serene, and yet her heart was anything but peaceful. Could that be a ship in the distance? No, it was just a figment of her imagination.

Her stomach rumbled.

How were her parents faring? Had they been told she was missing? Had Padi survived? She hoped so, if only to allow her the chance to throttle him. And Dake! The skunk! Using her research as a cover for treasure hunting. She wanted to get her hands on the loot if only to thwart him. What if he hired someone else to go after it when it became known she and Padi were lost at sea?

Her list of worries and grievances began to pile high and her mind raced to give each of them adequate attention. Forty days! She had too much to sort out! She could not sit around for forty days! What was God thinking?

Who is this who darkens counsel by words without knowledge? Now prepare yourself. I will question you, and you shall answer Me.

Nethania's brows shot upward in surprise as the voice of God rang clearly within her. The words were not audible. They were external thoughts that impressed themselves upon her mind and every syllable dripped with authority.

Where were you when I laid the foundations of the earth? Tell Me, if you have understanding. Who determined its measurements? Surely you know!

Nethania was mute.

Or who stretched the line upon it? To what were its foundations fastened? Or who laid its cornerstone, when the morning stars sang together, and all the sons of God shouted for joy? Or who shut in the sea with doors, when it burst forth and issued from the womb; when I made the clouds its garment, and thick darkness its swaddling band; when I fixed My limit for it, and set bars and doors; when I said, 'this far you may come, but no farther, and here your proud waves must stop!'

Have you commanded the morning since your days began, and caused the dawn to know its place, that it might take hold of the ends of the earth, and the wicked be shaken out of it?

Nethania swallowed hard and felt the finger of conviction upon her prideful heart. "No Papa, I haven't."

Have you entered the springs of the sea? Or have

you walked in search of the depths?

She felt instantly humbled. "No."

Have the gates of death been revealed to you? Or have you seen the doors of the shadow of death?

Her eyes lifted to the sky. "No."

Have you comprehended the breadth of the earth? Tell Me, if you know all this.

Her gaze dropped. "No Papa."

Where is the way to the dwelling of light? And darkness, where is its place, that you may take it to its territory, that you may know the paths to its home? Do you know it, because you were born then, or because the number of your days is great?

Tears of shame welled in her eyes.

Can you find the cluster of the Pleiades, or loose the belt of Orion? Can you bring out Mazzaroth in its season? Or can you guide the Great Bear with its cubs? Do you know the ordinances of the heavens? Can you set their dominion over the earth?

Nethania's eyes lifted once again to the sky. Although it was daylight, she drew from memory the vast starry host, innumerable should one even dare to count. She pictured in her mind what she knew of the universe beyond the blue orb she called home, envisioning stunning galaxies the Hubble telescope had shown mankind.

A shrinking feeling came over her. She was so small in comparison. Who was she to tell the Creator of those galaxies what to do? She could not even get off this island by herself.

"I'm sorry, Papa. Forgive me please?"

Can you lift up your voice to the clouds, that an abundance of water may cover you? Can you send out lightnings, that they may go, and say to you, 'Here we are!'?

Nethania bit her lower lip.

By worrying can you add one cubit to your stature?

Abased, she could say no more than, "No, my Father."

Therefore do not worry, saying, 'What shall we eat?' or 'What shall we drink?' or 'What shall we wear?' For after all these things the gentiles seek. For your heavenly Father knows that you need all these things. But seek first the kingdom of God and His righteousness, and all these things shall be added to you. Therefore do not worry about tomorrow, for tomorrow will worry about its own things. Sufficient for the day is its own trouble.

The familiar passage from Matthew chapter six took on a life of its own in context of her situation, and she felt a weight lift off her shoulders.

Judge not, that you be not judged. For with what judgement you judge, you will be judged; and with the same measure you use, it will be measured back to you.

Nethania thought of her friends at church and the way they had wrongfully treated her. The same old bitterness and anger rose to the surface. She had forgiven them yesterday, or had she? Yes, she had!

Frustration vied for position. Why did it have to be

so difficult? She was right back where she started! Her brows drew together thoughtfully, her unseeing gaze drifting across the water.

Perhaps forgiveness was a daily act and not just a once off thing? Before her musings could go further, more scriptures she had memorised as a teenager flooded her awareness.

And why do you look at the speck in your brother's eye, but do not consider the plank in your own eye? Or how can you say to your brother, 'Let me remove the speck out of your eye'; and look, a plank is in your own eye? Hypocrite! First remove the plank from your own eye, and then you will see clearly to remove the speck out of your brother's eye.

Nethania could not help feeling a little angry. She had been the victim! "Where was I at fault in what happened?"

There seemed to be silence from heaven. She waited.

Finally the scene from that hurtful day played before her mind's eye. This time, she saw what had happened as though outside of it all. She had been in the shower when there was a knock at the door. Aidan answered it wearing only a towel. When asked where she was, he had simply replied, *"In the shower."*

Her eyes widened and her stomach churned. Alana should not have assumed. All the same, it *had* looked bad. Alana had said nothing and promptly left.

Another verse from scripture unexpectedly floated through her mind.

Abstain from all appearance of evil.

She cringed. She had failed on that count. As Nethania lived at home with her family, she had not given it any thought. Although both hers and Aidan's motives and behaviour had been completely blameless, in the light of her moral stance, it had not been wise to clean up at her place without at least a family member home. It had given an opportunity for Alana to presume the worst, and no one had been able to speak on their behalf regarding their innocent behaviour. Not even Aidan's protests had changed their thinking.

She then remembered the bitterness, hatred and anger she had harboured for the past six months. All those years of conducting herself in an honourable manner and working hard to earn respect and credibility by living what she believed, had been lost in one moment of time.

No, she was by no means an innocent victim. She too had played her part. Nethania lifted her hands to the sky in humble supplication.

"I ask for You to forgive me, Father, and again I lay down my bitterness and anger. I choose to forgive and no longer to dwell on the hurts inflicted by Your people. May You give them the grace to do the same toward me?"

Peace washed over her soul in a refreshing wave and she smiled. Suddenly the water at the base of the rocks came alive with a riot of activity. A school of terrified fish started leaping clear of the surface in their bid to escape what appeared to be a bull shark on the hunt.

79

Nethania watched in amazement as several fish landed on the rocks and floundered helplessly. Her rumbling stomach was never far from her mind, and it spurred her into action. She pounced upon the closest scaly victim and managed to wrestle it into a small rock pool several metres behind her. She repeated the process, unable to suppress a giggle or two over the chaotic struggle, until she had four fat specimens captive.

Finally she stood and surveyed her catch and a smile of wonder over God's miraculous provision lit her face.

"I know for sure who controls the ocean and its wildlife."

She went to fetch her makeshift spear.

11

"I'm sorry to do this to you," Commander Sharni Sydenham said over the phone, "but the crew of a fishing charter found five bodies at sea."

Joshua sighed softly and leaned against the kitchen counter, the telephone receiver to his ear. "Isn't that a job for the coast guard or federal police?"

"The charter captain, Oliver Startori, believes they're refugees. There may be more in the area if a boat has gone down."

Surprise flicked Joshua's heart rate up a notch. "Ollie?"

"You know him?" The commander from headquarters sounded curious.

"Yes. He's ex-navy. He worked on The Hartfield for a few years. He's a good man." If Ollie believed the bodies were refugees then Joshua would not argue. "When do we sail?"

He dreaded the answer for Faith's sake. He knew Joey would understand. She had been in the navy and was familiar with the demands of the job.

"An hour. Your crew is being recalled as we speak."

Joshua cringed. Would they all be sober? The night was still young, so he assumed they would be. "I expect Navcom will brief me in more detail within the hour?"

"Yes. I'll be in touch."

"Thank you Commander." Joshua hung up and ran a tentative hand through his short black hair. It was time to tell Joey. He cringed at the prospect and sighed in resignation. One of these days he would receive a promotion and hopefully a shore posting.

He wandered reluctantly toward the living room and stopped in the doorway. He met his wife's gaze across the room. Linc was standing and tapping out a text on his cell phone.

"You don't have to look so sheepish, Josh." Joey's eyes gleamed with sudden amusement. "Linc just got a message. You've been crash sailed."

Joshua crossed to the couch and leaned down to kiss her gently on the mouth. "I'm sorry."

She smiled warmly. "I understand. You can apologise like that some more when you return."

He grinned. "Deal." He claimed one more before going to fetch his duffle bag. Thankfully he hadn't unpacked yet.

~

Linc felt torn as he stared at his baby girl asleep in Joey's arms. He hated to leave her so soon. At the same time, it was a relief. He ached over Tessa and the huge responsibility of caring for Yasmin was burdening him at a time when he could barely think straight. Yet a piece of him desperately needed to keep Yasmin close, and in so doing, hold a part of Tessa.

"I'll take good care of her, Linc."

He met Joey's gaze in surprise. Astute moon shaped eyes steadily held his. She had accurately read him again. His lips tipped up at one end.

"Thanks Joey. I guess I'll see you either late tonight or early tomorrow morning."

"When you get back, plan to crash here for a few days."

Linc instantly rebelled. He wanted to take her up on the offer. In fact, he needed to. He was also very aware of what a huge imposition that would be. "I can't do that to you all Joey."

"It wasn't a request sailor." Her dark eyes took on a steely glint. "It was an order."

Linc almost laughed at the absurdity of such a small woman ordering a big, independent bloke like him around. Almost. He knew he would not win in an argument with Joey Donnelly.

"Yes ma'am." He gave her an amused smile and dropped a kiss on her cheek. "I'll see you later."

Joey smiled in satisfaction. "I'll have the spare room ready."

Linc held one of Yasmin's tiny hands with mixed emotions. He smoothed her tiny brow and said good-bye. He had a short time in which to fetch his duffle and report for duty.

~

Daylight had vanished by the time The Hartfield arrived to collect the bodies. Dayne and Ollie had spent the day diving with the young holidaying couple, although their cargo was never far from mind.

Lon and Coz, along with Farmer, came over in a RHIB. They photographed and then bagged the bodies. The transfer was made in a relatively short time and Ollie was allowed to go. He bid his mates aboard The Hartfield goodbye and set sail for port.

His mind, however, could not let go of the questions surrounding the mysterious death of the refugee family.

~

The officers not required on the bridge were all in attendance in the ship's office that night for a debriefing. As the meeting was coming to a close, Shep voiced the question uppermost on Linc's mind.

"How do you suppose they died?"

"That's for the coroner to find out."

"I had Jaffa print the photos I took." Farmer drew the pictures from an envelope and splayed them across the table.

Both Wilko and Lon sifted through them, obviously looking for some clue to the mystery. Linc's gaze landed upon the disturbing images and he felt sick. He had seen dead bodies before, but never had he lost someone so close to him for it to have such an impact.

His thoughts swung immediately to Tessa and reality crashed down around him. She was dead too. Buried. Lifeless. Gone forever. The finality of it struck him like a blow to the face.

Suddenly anger raged within him at the rude confrontation with death. He sprang from his seat and stormed from the room, slamming the door shut upon his exit.

~

"What's up with the X?" Shep's stunned gaze lingered on the closed door.

His was not the only astonished expression in the room. The executive officer was a squared away sailor. Displays of temper and breaches of protocol were not in his character.

Compassion tightened Joshua's chest. "The lieutenant lost someone close to him and has only just found out about it today."

Lon and Shep exchanged worried glances. Farmer looked instantly contrite and gathered the photographs.

"Is there anything we can do?" Wilko asked.

Joshua appreciated the way his people cared for one another. "Just give him some space for now. I'll talk to him." He returned to the business at hand. "The search for any other refugees or a boat in the area is complete, so the ship will dock in an hour, all going well. If there's nothing else, you're all free to go."

A furrow remained in Wilko's brow. "Sir, is there any word on a replacement for Corey Knight?"

Joshua sighed and mentally kicked himself. "Sorry Wilko, with all that's been going on I forgot to tell you. HMAS Melbourne is sending us one of their grease monkeys. A sailor called Jonesy."

Wilko nodded with satisfaction. "'Bout time. Is he any good?"

Joshua leaned back casually in his chair. "Don't know. The guy's only been in the navy three years and apparently his contract will be up in a few months. All the same, we'll take what we can get."

Wilko shrugged. "Guess a rookie's better than nothin'."

"If that's all, dismissed." Joshua fought the urge to yawn.

"Thank you sir." Wilko nodded.

One by one the officers filed from the room. Joshua went in search of Linc.

12

"I'm sorry I lost it sir." Linc was sitting against the metal casing of the port side crane used for launching the RHIB.

It had taken Joshua a good ten minutes to track him down to the quarter deck. He sank to the floor beside him. "I understand."

Silence fell. The sky above them twinkled brightly, and a calm sea stretched to the horizon to meet it.

"I need to take some time off sir." Linc's troubled gaze followed the churning trail left in The Hartfield's wake.

Joshua nodded thoughtfully. "I think you should. In fact, I was about to suggest it."

Linc smiled ruefully. "I was unprofessional back there."

Joshua rested his elbows on his bent knees. "That's not why I think you should take a break."

Linc cast him a curious sidelong glance.

"Your reaction was just a symptom. You're still in shock. You need to come to grips with losing Tessa and becoming a father. It won't happen in a day. You've got grief to deal with and big adjustments to make. It's going to take time, and frankly, all of that has precedence over the navy. I've been there."

"How did you deal with losing your wife?"

Joshua could sense the desperation in his friend for some kind of direction. He well remembered not knowing what to do with the pain, and feeling it so strongly that it was like a vice squeezing his chest.

"Trust me when I tell you you don't want to follow my example."

Linc's curious gaze lingered on his. "Why not?"

"I got angry at the world and pushed away everyone I loved. Then I buried myself in work. It wasn't until Joey introduced me to Jesus that true healing came." Joshua remembered the comfort he had experienced when he had understood his first wife's faith in Christ, and consequently her eternal destination. He had known then that it was not goodbye forever.

"How could Jesus possibly help? He died over two thousand years ago."

Joshua studied his friend inquisitively. How much did he know about God and His rescue plan for mankind? "It's true that Jesus died," he hedged carefully. "But He didn't stay dead. You see, God had a plan and his Son's death was just the beginning."

"You've lost me," Linc stated flatly.

Joshua let his gaze wander to the ocean, which was as vast as the love of the One Who had made it. "Joey explained it like this: God is holy and His standards are exceptionally high. He holds us accountable for every-thing we've ever said or done, even down to the things we think. He's got the right to. He's God. Unfortunately the punishment for breaking God's standards is death and hell. It's not what He wants, but to reward sin any other way would make Him an unjust judge."

Joshua knew Linc understood about law and judgement. From what he had gleaned of his past, that had been all he had received from his family. Joshua could even see his friend recoiling from the God they were discussing, likely as a result of his parents' poor treatment of him in the Father's name.

"God came up with a plan to save His people from that fate. A plan that would also satisfy His requirement that justice be served. Jesus would take the punishment of death and hell, and so meet God's requirement that sin's cost be paid. Being sinless, He was the perfect sacrifice."

Joshua easily read the revulsion on his comrade's face. "Make no mistake Linc, God loved His Son. Jesus had the opportunity to refuse, but He didn't. The Bible says that Jesus endured the cross, because set before Him was the joy that would be His when you and me, and as many as would believe and follow Him, would join Him in heaven.

"You see, Jesus didn't stay dead, and if He had, faith in Him would be pointless. It would make Him just like every other prophet who has claimed to have the way to eternal life, and yet ended up in the grave. Jesus was different. He rose again three days after His crucifixion, making Him the first of many to rise from death to eternal life in heaven.

"Amanda, my wife, was a follower of Jesus. When I met Him too and asked forgiveness for my sins, He stamped 'paid in full' upon the debt that would have dragged me to hell. Now my name is written in Jesus' Book of Life, and one day I will join Him in heaven. I'll see Amanda again, and the comfort that brings is matchless."

Linc paled and Joshua wondered at what Tessa's beliefs had been.

"What about those who don't believe?"

Linc's question said a lot, and Joshua's heart overflowed with compassion. "God chases a soul till it's last breath. God was with Tess when she died. Only He knows what she did with Him in her final moments. I'm concerned about you. You still have time, and you've yet to respond to Christ's gift of love and mercy. Don't leave it too late, Linc." Sensing the conversation had come to a close, he quietly rose.

He had given Linc much to meditate on, and he left him there deep in thought.

~

Amelia Jones sat her navy blue duffle on the dock and looked the Armidale boat over from bow to stern. Her apprehensive gaze lifted to the tinted windows of the bridge. How would the crew receive her?

On the Melbourne she'd been able to blend into the background with its size and the large number of sailors aboard. This was, in contrast, a very small boat with a crew of only twenty-one. If anyone decided they didn't like her, then she would have no place of escape.

Amelia swallowed hard and picked up her bag.

"Please God, help me to do an outstanding job, for Your name's sake?"

She took her first steps toward the gangway. She saluted the white ensign flag flying on the quarter deck and boarded.

~

"You're who?" Wilko called above the noise in the engine room.

He wiped his greasy hands on an old rag and stared down at the diminutive woman. It would be generous to say the top of her head came to his collar bone. Her curly brown hair was pulled back into a pony tail and stray wisps had been tucked beneath a navy issue cap. Freckles stood out upon a delicate nose and hazel eyes regarded him uncertainly. He wouldn't call her striking or beautiful, but she was rather cute.

"Seaman Jones sir." She cringed at an unnatural noise accompanying the usual burble of the engines.

Wilko also noted the unhealthy sound and turned to a tall sailor tinkering with one of the two diesels. "Cut it!"

His lanky assistant obeyed and the room went quiet. Wilko returned his attention to the small woman in uniform standing just inside the hatch.

He tucked a corner of a rag into his belt. "What were

you saying?"

"Seaman Jones, sir, reporting for duty," she spoke softly, seeming embarrassed by her first failed attempt at an introduction.

Wilko's brows hiked almost to his hairline. "You're Jonesy?"

She nodded with wide innocent eyes. He snorted in semi amusement.

"What's the navy doin' to me?" He indicated his assistant with a thumb over his shoulder. "This is Leading Seaman Debartista and I'm Chief Petty Officer Wilkinson. Down here it's Ron an' Wilko."

She nodded again, her gaze straying hesitantly to the young man. She offered him a timid smile. An amused one tugged at Ron's lips and he exchanged glances with the chief engineer.

"The duty watchman explained that while the ship is docked for a few days, you're giving the engines a tune-up," she offered. "I'm not due to report for a couple of days, but I thought you might like an extra pair of hands." She shrugged and looked hopeful she might be put to work.

For the first time since hearing she was the replacement, Wilko was optimistic. He liked a hard worker. "You any good?"

Jonesy's head tilted and a challenge sparkled in her eyes. "There's only one way to find out."

He grinned. "I like your attitude."

She broke eye contact and surveyed the two engines, which were almost three metres in length, and close to one and a half metres in width. "MTU sixteen cylinder M-seventy diesels. That sound before... Were you thinking it might be related to the crank shaft?"

Wilko and Ron glanced at each other again.

"Yeah. The crank shaft core plugs need a check as well." He was intrigued when her eyes passed over the engines appreciatively.

"When was it last cleaned and gauged?" Clearly her mind was already problem solving.

Ron had not picked up the problem as quickly as Jonesy had. His astute mind made a few assessments.

"That was my next move. If you've got time, I could use ya."

She nodded decisively. "Good. Where do you want me to start?"

"You can check the valves." Wilko watched a satisfied look come over her cute little face as she went straight to work. He felt a twinge of uncertainty. She could talk the talk, but could she cut it with a wrench?

13

Linc was at his bungalow the following morning packing a few extra belongings when there was a knock at the door. He wondered which of the boys had dropped by and mentally squirmed. He really wasn't up to dealing with company.

He opened the front door and stared in wonder. Looking back were two familiar brown eyes tinged by anxiety. Blond hair framed her lovely face and fell past her shoulders in straight locks. She looked just like their mother.

His thoughts tumbled over one another in an astonished jumble. "Jaclyn, what are you doing here?"

His sister frowned in concern. "I was hoping you could answer that. The message you left me yesterday has me worried."

Linc was astounded. "You flew across the country to check if I'm alright?"

Jaclyn's eyes began to shine with the tell tale Hobbs mischievous gleam. "May I come in?"

Her question brought Linc out of his stunned stupor. He stepped across the threshold and gathered her into a strong embrace. "I am *so* glad you're here!"

Jaclyn's eyes widened in surprise at his fierce reaction, and he figured he would have to explain. For now he was just grateful she had come.

~

Ron's cry brought Amelia's head up instantly where it collided with the engine block. She winced, stood, and rubbed the knot forming on her skull. She moved around the starboard engine until her workmates came into view.

"What's the matter?" The men had no trouble hearing her voice, as her volume was amplified by alarm.

Ron was standing by the port diesel clutching his arm and gritting his teeth. Wilko pried his fingers loose and studied the red welt quickly forming on the younger man's arm.

"You know some parts of the engine get hot when it's running. You should've been more careful!"

"Yeah, I know."

Amelia sighed with relief. It was just a burn. It could have been a severed finger or hand. She shared Wilko's irritation, while at the same time she sympathised. She'd burned herself once too. That had been sufficient for her to learn her lesson.

"Come on." Wilko started toward the hatch. "We'll get some cold water on it then take you to casualty."

Ron kept his lips clamped shut. Amelia wondered if he might be trying not to swear. Wilko had told him off twice that morning for using foul language in the presence of a lady, something that intrigued her.

She watched them go and compassion tugged at her heart. Aware there was nothing she could do, she went back to her task. She was methodically working through the list Wilko had made, and when she finished her current task, she went on to complete what the men had started.

~

"She is so adorable Linc!" Jaclyn was cuddling her niece that evening.

Linc was beside her on the Donnelly's couch. Joshua and Joey were putting Faith to bed, and Linc could hear them singing children's songs and laughing from where he sat. He smiled at the soft and silly side to his commanding officer.

He looked at his sister, and something that had been on his mind often came once again to the fore. He studied her carefully and concluded he would have to be blind to miss it.

"Jackie, what happened five years ago that changed you?"

She sent him a surprised sideways glance, and he thought it might be because he had never brought up the subject. She shifted to face him and drew her legs up onto the couch. Yasmin's eyelids opened and closed sleepily several more times. She would doze off any minute. Jaclyn smiled, and then met Linc's gaze.

"It's a long story."

He was intrigued by the serenity that seemed to envelop her. "I want to know."

"I was thirteen when you left home. Mum and Dad were so mad at you for the choices you'd made. They broke off contact and basically washed their hands of you."

Tears spilled onto her lashes and they wrung Linc's already frayed heart.

"They forbade me to write or call and things stayed like that for years. I was too scared to disobey. Then I turned eighteen, moved out and looked you up. I'm so sorry I went along with how they treated you, but at the time I didn't know I had a choice."

Linc stared into his sister's anguished face and felt tears sting the back of his eyes. "I'd hoped that was all that kept you away, and not the things I'd done."

"Linc, you were young. When you saw where it was taking you, you signed up with the navy and straightened your life out. Besides, if what Mum and Dad had was real, they would never have cut you off."

Linc studied her curiously. "What do you mean?"

Jaclyn quietly assessed him. He figured she found what she must have been searching for when she started to go into detail.

"When I moved out, I lived with a friend. She was big into church and God and at first I wondered if I might have landed in a worse predicament than before. But then I watched her life and the way she treated people, and I had to admit that her faith was real. Her God was powerful and very much at work in her life."

Jaclyn's thoughtful gaze drifted unseeingly across the room. "She believed one hundred percent in what the Bible said and didn't compromise. At the same time, she didn't judge or criticise or punish others who fell short. She was humble when she failed and honest to a fault.

"What struck me most was her compassion, and the grace and mercy she showed to everyone." Jaclyn met Linc's open gaze and seemed heartened. "It was because of her that I decided to begin a relationship with Jesus too. I know what I have in Him is real, and He's taken away my fear."

Linc could not deny that something inside her had altered. As a child, she had been a quivering bundle of nerves. When he'd left, he had wished to take her with him. He'd wanted to protect her and give her a place where she was free to be herself.

"Thanks for telling me." With those words, he closed the conversation on spiritual matters. He needed time to think.

14

It was close to nine that evening when Wilko returned to the ship. He had waited several hours in casualty, which was overrun with patients. He had finally taken Ron home when his arm had been treated.

He trudged wearily up the stairway to the bridge feeling disgruntled at how far behind they would be due to Ron's misfortune. Tyson Rossetti heard his approach and scooted out of the captain's chair. Wilko appeared a moment later and Tyso saluted. The chief engineer's return salute was considerably lacking in enthusiasm.

"As you were, Tys. Slow night?" He dreaded the long hours he would have to pull to get maintenance back on schedule. He was stalling.

Tyson dropped back into the captain's chair. "Yep. Jamie's due back from his routine check, and port security will call on the hour. That's about it. How's Ron?"

"Sleeping like a baby thanks to the painkillers. He'll be alright, although I can't say the same for me. I might end up doin' an all nighter at this rate." Wilko propped his hands on his hips. "The rookie... When did she clock off?"

Tyson leaned casually in his chair and re-opened his hunting magazine. "She came up to let the watch know she was finished at seven-thirty. She left a note on your desk." Tyson pointed a thumb over his shoulder, indicating the engineer's station tucked away at the rear of the bridge. He suddenly smiled and turned to Wilko.

"She brought us dinner too. Some kind of rice dish she rustled up in the galley. She said she left some in the fridge for you and Ron." Tyson looked thoughtful. "She's a nice girl. Real shy an' quiet, but nice."

Wilko was surprised. She had worked late and also cooked for the duty watch? He wandered to his desk and found the note his comrade had mentioned. He glanced over it, not knowing quite what to expect. He exhaled and his brows rose in incredulity as he scanned the maintenance list the three of them had been working from. All but two tasks had been crossed off. Beneath them was an apology.

'Sorry sir, but I couldn't get the rest done. I was getting hungry. I'll make it up to you tomorrow.'

Wilko shook his head. Did she think there was another list? She had whittled the only one down significantly. His mind grew suspicious and his lips pressed grimly together. Had she cut corners?

List still in hand, he made his way into the ship's belly. There he carefully went over each engine, cross checking the list with the finished product. After ruthless scrutiny, he finally stepped back and scratched his head. He could not fault her work. The Melbourne had sent him their best.

~

Leading Seaman Jamie Oldham stopped mid stride down the passage and did a double-take. He back tracked and took a better look in the junior sailor's mess. He had finished his security check and was heading to the bridge.

However, curled up fast asleep on her side along a cushioned bench beside the fixed table was Jonesy. Jamie stepped inside and studied her for several silent minutes. Her head was pillowed on her duffle bag and oil smudges had found their way onto her forehead, nose and cheeks. Her hands, although likely washed, did not look much better. An empty bowl sat on the table where she had eaten.

Jamie wondered why she hadn't gone straight to bed if she was so tired. Her cap was hooked to her right pant pocket and loose wisps of shoulder length, curly brown hair had escaped to tickle her freckled nose.

He smiled. She was cute in a teddy bear kind of way. He gently shook her. "Jonesy."

She did not stir and he tried again.

"Jonesy, wake up."

She roused and blinked in confusion at her surroundings. She sat up slowly and rubbed what had to be a stiff neck. She stared blearily at Jamie and he could not resist an amused smile at her adorable dishevelled look.

"Sorry to wake you, but you'd be better off in your rack."

Jonesy's cheeks heated in embarrassment. "I don't have one yet. When I came on board there was no one to show me which berth was mine. It wasn't a problem 'cos all I wanted to do at the time was get to work." She shuffled out from the bench and stood.

Jamie smiled. "Come on, I'll show you. You'll bunk with Switch and Katie. They're the only other girls on board by the way." He stepped into the corridor.

Jonesy collected her bag and reached for her bowl.

"Leave it. I'll do the dishes later."

"Are you sure?"

He kept a straight face, although he could not suppress a teasing gleam. "No, that's why I offered."

Jonesy caught the cheeky sparkle in his eyes and smiled shyly. She left the bowl and followed him.

15

Linc stood by Tessa's grave. A brisk wind tussled his brown hair. Dark clouds overshadowed the cemetery. He felt cold inside, as though the weather had infiltrated his very soul.

Was Tessa gone forever, or was she with Jesus in heaven?

"What choice did you make, babe?"

His question was whisked away by the wind, unanswered. Maybe there was no heaven or hell? Was he willing to stake his eternity on it?

No.

Linc considered himself a logical man, and to disregard the possibility he might be wrong would be foolhardy. Still, he needed more evidence if he was to place his life in the hands of Jesus Christ.

His eyes lifted to the sky and he offered his first prayer in over ten years. "Jesus, if you're really alive like Josh says, show me somehow? Because if You are and You're as good as Jackie claims, I'd like to meet You."

The clouds suddenly parted and brilliant sunshine burst through. One large ray beamed directly upon him, warm and comforting. Yet not even the sun could compete with the warmth that touched his grief-chilled heart. Linc was not a man who placed much stock in emotions. However, he could not deny the force of the love wrapping itself around him in that moment. If this was God, he wanted to stay in His embrace forever.

"Okay, You're real."

Tears rolled down his cheeks as the love pressed closer. It beckoned entrance to his soul. At the same time, shame welled within him. He would be a fool to say he had no sin. The purity of the Presence around him convinced him of that fact. Linc hated the things in his life keeping the love at arm's reach.

"I'm sorry Jesus. I'm sorry for not living up to Your standards. I'm sorry for drunken brawls and reckless driving as a youngster. I'm sorry I didn't wait for marriage. I'm sorry for hating my parents and causing them so much heartache. I'm sorry for my pride and self reliance."

Linc went on to confess every wrong thing that came to mind from his past and his present, until finally the love swirling around him in a rapturous vortex whispered through him and settled down to stay.

Linc closed his eyes and more tears fell. This time they sprang from matchless comfort. It was something he had never experienced before, and knew he would not be able to explain if he tried.

~

Jaclyn watched her brother anxiously as he walked in

the Donnelly's front door that evening. She was aware he had planned to visit Tessa's grave for the first time, and when he hadn't returned for hours, she had become worried.

Joshua was on the floor doing a large wooden puzzle with Faith. Jaclyn rose from an armchair and passed him baby Yasmin. She wordlessly crossed the room and met Linc where he stood quietly in the doorway.

"You met Him." It was a statement.

Tears clouded his green eyes and a serene smile played about his mouth. Obviously overwhelmed and unable to form any words, he simply nodded. Jaclyn laughed in wonder and hugged him fiercely.

"Met who?" Joey wandered from the kitchen.

"Jesus!" Jaclyn beamed and stepped away. "He met Jesus. Just look at him!"

She pointed to his shining face and wanted to laugh and cry at the same time.

"You did what?" Joey suddenly let loose an excited scream and flung her arms around him.

Linc laughed over her exuberance. Joshua chuckled and carried Yasmin to her father. Faith joined them and a lively celebration began.

~

Nethania sat up and rubbed her back. She glared at the nasty vine that had caught her foot, causing her to land on a protruding tree root. She followed its full length into the forest canopy where something yellow caught her eye.

"How about that! And to think I've been living off fish when you've been there all along."

She stood and rubbed her lower back one more time while considering how to go about fetching some bananas from the bunches thriving above her. If they were growing here, she wondered what other fruits she might find. Her smile broadened and she silently marvelled.

Papa, You've got me living like a queen on this island!

She grasped a sturdy vine and used it to pull herself into the tree closest to the ripe yellow fruit.

~

Amelia pressed the start button on the washing machine and frowned when nothing happened. She checked the power switch. It was on. Why wasn't it working?

She had transferred from The Melbourne in the clothes she stood in and only a few changes in her duffle. After the last two days' work, her uniforms were close to being massacred. She certainly couldn't wander around in civilian attire when the crew arrived tomorrow for duty.

She removed her clothes from the machine and began to pull the thing apart to assess the problem.

~

Wilko scratched his head and puzzled over the disappearance of his toolbox. His stomach rumbled. He had yet to shower and change for dinner at Lon's place.

He shrugged off the mystery and strode toward his berth. Clunking and clattering came from the laundry and halted him in his tracks. Who, beside the duty watch, was still around at this hour?

He eased open the laundry door and peered suspiciously inside. His brows rose in surprise. His toolbox was on the floor and a pair of legs were sticking out from behind the washing machine.

"Are you haunting this ship Jonesy?"

Amelia jerked with fright and a resounding thud made Wilko cringe. She emerged from between the wall and the machine, screw driver in one hand and the other clutching her head. She winced and looked up at him standing in the doorway.

"Sorry kid. You okay?" A rogue gleam of humour dampened the sincerity in his eyes.

She gave him a sheepish grin. "That's the second time I've done that in two days."

"Is that machine still acting up?" Switch, Leading Seaman Sarah Young, was supposed to have fixed the offending appliance several days ago.

"Not for long." Determination laced Amelia's declaration.

Wilko was inclined to agree with Jamie's description of their new engineer. Stray wisps of hair had escaped her ponytail to frame her oil smudged face and tickle her freckled nose. The words teddy bear did indeed come to mind.

Amelia took another minute to tweak the motor. Wilko leaned against the door frame and crossed his arms, curious about the outcome. She re-emerged, dropped the screwdriver back into the metal chest and stood. She wriggled her fingers theatrically over the buttons and closed her eyes. She held her breath and pressed start. The machine came to life and she sighed with satisfaction and smiled.

"That's more like it."

Wilko had a chuckle. "Magic fingers hey?"

She grinned at him. "More like prayerful ones."

He was instantly intrigued. "What are you doing for dinner tonight?"

"Most likely scrounging around in the galley. Why?"

"That won't do. Get scrubbed up kid. You're comin' with me."

Amelia's uncertain gaze met his. He wondered at the alarm he thought he read. She surprised him in the next moment by being straight forward about what was troubling her.

"My old shipmates took me clubbing once and I felt awkward and uncomfortable all night. Bars and clubs aren't really my scene. I promised myself I'd never let myself be pressured into going somewhere I don't feel safe again, even if it means staying on board during liberty." She avoided his gaze during her speech, and glanced up briefly, presumably to see if she had upset him with her frankness.

Wilko's eyes gleamed with humour, and renewed respect. He liked that she had steel in her backbone.

"Lon and his wife invited me to dinner at their place. Lon's the bosun. We were gunna watch the footy. Carrie'll be glad for another woman to chat with."

Amelia visibly relaxed and smiled in gratitude. "Thank you Wilko. I'll clean up."

She left and he gave the repaired machine a final glance and shook his head. He would be sure to inform the captain they were onto a winner and ensure they kept her.

16

Joey and Joshua went to bed early, leaving the two night owls in the living room to talk. Jaclyn was reclining in an armchair opposite the sofa. Linc was stretched out on the couch on his back cuddling his daughter. Jaclyn studied the pink bundle asleep on her father's broad chest and smiled. Just like Linc, she had fallen in love with the baby girl and would do anything for her. Jaclyn's choice had come easily and it was time she discussed it with her brother.

"What are your plans, Linc?"

He turned his head on the cushion to see her. "I have no idea."

Despite the uncertainty in his life, he seemed peaceful. God's love was obviously still carrying him through the dark valley of grief.

"Do you want a shore posting?"

Linc's gaze returned to Yasmin on her stomach atop his chest. Her tiny arms were spread wide above her head and her right cheek was pressed against him.

"No, but I'll do whatever I have to to keep her." His large hand engulfed her back.

"I have something I want to suggest and I'm hoping you'll consider it."

Linc looked across at her curiously.

110

Jaclyn licked suddenly dry lips. "What would you say to me moving in with you for a while?" She hurried on to explain before he could interject with the objection so clearly on his tongue. "I would care for Yasmin while you're at sea and you wouldn't have to give up your job."

"Yeah, but what about your life? I can't expect you to just give up everything for me."

Jaclyn's gaze warmed as she beheld her niece. The poor little character needed a mother, and the closest thing at this point in time was an adoring aunt.

"Something tells me I won't be giving up a thing. Besides, I can continue my work editing from Cairns just as easily as I can in Perth."

Linc stared at her for several silent minutes. "You would do that for me?"

Jaclyn smiled affectionately at her brother. "I'd move to the ends of the earth if you needed me."

His eyes misted and he looked away.

"Linc?"

Several moments passed in silence and she saw him swallow hard. He was fighting a tumult of emotions. Finally he nodded and a pleased smile claimed Jaclyn's lips.

"Good. I'll make the arrangements."

~

Bruno Dizane glanced sideways with a smug smile at

his first mate, Cliff Garvey. The man gave a pragmatic shrug. The money was clearly a big draw.

Bruno was curious. "Why don't ya hire a fishin' charter?"

Garvey's murky brown eyes took on a distrustful glint. "Yeah, why us?"

Padi sat opposite the two fishermen in the small Cairns pub. The room was alive with the evening crowd watching football on the large screen TV on the far wall, playing pool, and socialising over a cool drink. They were at a small table in the centre of the room, surrounded by easy going locals.

Padi hated to admit why he had chosen the run down vessel with a rough looking crew, but he was desperate. The money was almost gone and Dake was breathing down his neck after his first failed voyage.

"I have little money."

Bruno snorted and half smiled. Both men lost interest and Garvey began to rise.

"Wait!" Padi felt distress mounting. "I give you percentage of what I find."

Dake would not be pleased, but even he was running low on funds after their recent debacle. Bruno motioned for Garvey to sit down. The skipper leaned back casually in his chair, the front legs lifting a couple of inches off the floor while he assessed Padi.

"Just what are ya lookin' for?"

~

"How did you end up in the navy Amelia?" Carrie Lonigan rested her chin on her palm and her elbow on the dining table. She studied her guest with interest.

The roar of the football crowd and the commentator on the television in the lounge room filled the house. The two men watching added their own commentary.

Amelia sipped her second cup of coffee and smiled at the lovely blond opposite her. "I finished high school and tried to get an apprenticeship in mechanics and was continually knocked back."

Carrie smiled and Amelia thought she could make a pretty good guess why. Amelia was small of stature and looked like she'd barely be able to lift a wrench let alone use it to work on an engine. Her eyes sparkled with humour in return.

"I suppose I didn't look like I could cut it. Anyway, for six years I worked at whatever came my way. Sales assistant, cleaner, sidekick for a landscaper. You name it, I did it. My desire to tinker with mechanics only grew. I figured in the end my only shot at it was if I joined the navy." She smiled and shrugged. "They took me. I went through training and ended up serving just shy of three years on The Melbourne.

"The Hartfield needed an extra body and my CO asked if I'd be willing to fill the gap." Her gaze drifted thoughtfully. "I can't think why God would uproot me like this, but I sensed it was what He wanted so I said yes. I'm trusting He knows best."

Carrie smiled warmly. "I'm sure He does." She

winked. "I'm kind of hoping you stick around awhile."

Amelia's heart warmed and she chuckled. "That's really kind."

"You've already made quite an impression on Wilko and my husband."

Amelia's embarrassed gaze dropped and her cheeks turned a light shade of pink. She never knew what to do with praise.

"So, where are you staying?"

She relaxed and her gaze lifted. "Aboard The Hartfield at the moment."

"You haven't found a place yet?"

Amelia shook her head and drank the last of her coffee. Her eyes felt leaden and her body was weary. Not even the caffeine was having any effect. "No. I only just transferred and who knows where I'll end up in three months when my contract is up."

"Do you have any family?"

Carrie's curious question was clearly aimed indirectly at Amelia's relationship status, and the other woman smiled in amusement.

"My parents, who I live with when I'm home. I have two bossy brothers who are both older. They're married and have kids. They all live in the tiny country town of Heyworth. It's about an hour and a half from Melbourne."

"Tell me about them?"

Amelia was surprised by Carrie's interest, and wondered if she had a close family. She began to tell her new friend about her loved ones and their quirky ways.

It was nearing midnight when Carrie suggested she and Wilko stay over and travel into work with Lon in the morning.

Wilko took the couch and Amelia the spare room. As she drifted off to sleep, her heart rejoiced that even though she was far from home, God had placed her in a family. His family.

17

"The coroner's report said the whole family died from eating a poisonous berry."

Ollie turned off the engine of his charter boat. He rose from the chair at the helm and turned to Dayne in the doorway. His friend had his hands on his hips and was regarding him with a grave expression.

"How did you get access to the coroner's report?"

Ollie grinned and brushed past him. He strode onto the main deck and dropped the anchor over the side. "I have connections in odd places."

Dayne followed him to the stern where a dingy was tied to the railing. "Just what are you planning to find on Finlay Island?"

Ollie climbed into the inflatable and took up an oar. Dayne, although still looking perplexed, stepped into the dingy and reached for the second oar. Off their starboard side roughly one hundred metres across crystal clear tropical waters, Finlay Island rose from the azure deep. A thin strip of white sand girded its steep jungle covered hillside. It was one of three uninhabited islands grouped near the Great Barrier Reef. Each island was visible from their boat bobbing gently in the coral sea.

"Some clue to what really happened to that family. They had to have been shipwrecked near here and possibly marooned on one of these islands. They're the only landmass within kilometres. It's possible more survivors from the sunken refugee boat made it to shore."

The men began rowing toward the sandy beach.

"But why build a raft and try to get off the island?"

Ollie glanced at the inhospitable jungle-covered mountain reaching for the sky. "They were sick and knew no help was going to reach them. It's my guess they took a chance a ship might pick them up, or at the most optimistic, they may have hoped to reach the mainland."

"That's insanity!"

Ollie's countenance darkened with sadness. "Yeah well, people will do crazy things when they're desperate."

"Like crossing the ocean in a leaky boat." Sympathy touched Dayne's features.

Ollie understood the response. He had seen and rescued many refugees fleeing their turbulent homelands in search of a dream. He had come across many who hadn't survived. From what he knew of Dayne, his parents had escaped Hungary as youths when it had come under communist rule.

The bow of the inflatable finally nudged the shore and the men leapt into the shallow water and pulled it further onto the sand. The beach was pristine. Ollie could not help but admire its untouched beauty.

Dayne's eyes followed the incline at the edge of the

sand. "Now what?"

The island reminded Ollie of a sombrero. "We go for a walk and take a look around." He sent Dayne his usual carefree smile.

His friend lifted a shoulder in an easy-going gesture and they wandered into the jungle together.

~

"We're happy to have you aboard, Jonesy." The captain smiled in genuine appreciation. "Wilko speaks highly of you."

Amelia stood at ease, hands behind her back. The Hartfield was making its way out of port. She had been summoned so that the commanding officer could meet the new sailor under his command. Despite her calm exterior, nervous butterflies engaged in somersaults inside her belly.

"The petty officer is a kind man." She was pleased by the compliment but also terribly uncomfortable being in the spotlight.

Five other sailors were listening in on the exchange from their stations on the bridge. Lieutenant Yates, the acting executive officer, was nearby, as was the radio operator, navigator, helmsman and Wilko at the marine link console.

Amelia just wanted to crawl under the nearest table and hide. Instead she offered a shy smile. "Is that all sir?"

Lieutenant Commander Donnelly seemed to read her discomfort and kindly dismissed her. Amelia sighed with relief and saluted. The captain reciprocated and she was released from the conversation to make a quick exit.

~

Ollie's saddened gaze passed over the bodies lying in a makeshift camp not twenty paces inland. There was nothing gruesome about their appearance. All seven seemed to have simply gone to sleep.

"They're families. Just like the one we found." Dayne's expression was dark. "They came so far and for what? This?"

The men were standing on the edge of camp surveying the heartbreaking scene. Ollie fought back tears and silently moved from one body to the next, checking for any signs of life. He reached the last person, a young Sri Lankan woman curled up on her side beside a man he presumed was her husband. He had no pulse, just like all the others.

Ollie placed two fingers alongside the woman's main artery in her neck. He was startled when she groaned and stirred.

"This woman is alive!"

Dayne moved swiftly to Ollie's side.

"Can you carry her to the inflatable while I finish sweeping the area? I want to make sure there's no one else."

Although pale, Dayne absorbed the grim scene in stoic silence. From what little he understood of his friend's past, Ollie was aware that death was not new to Dayne.

He gently lifted the sick woman. She moaned softly and opened her eyes.

"Sh, we'll get you to a doctor soon." He carried her toward the beach.

Ollie scanned the area and walked the camp perimetre. Something rustled in the undergrowth to his right and he paused mid stride.

He scanned the tangle of vines in the trees. He caught a shape incongruent with the landscape. His gaze swung back for a second look. Two large brown eyes stared at him from behind a gnarled trunk. Short black hair fell across a caramel coloured forehead.

Ollie's heart leapt into his throat. A child had survived. He appeared to be Sri Lankan. All but two of the refugees seemed to be middle eastern. This little boy must belong to the woman who was alive.

Ollie squatted down to the child's level and looked into his frightened eyes. He was no more than five metres away, hiding at the edge of camp.

Ollie used a gentle tone. "You can come out. I won't hurt you. I want to help."

He extended his hand and offered a smile. He ached for all the little tyke had suffered. The boy regarded him with suspicion. Ollie kept his hand extended and his voice kind.

"Please come out?"

The child stepped away from the trunk and hesitated.

"Come on." He offered another smile.

The boy scrutinised him for several silent minutes and must have decided he could be trusted. He walked forward. Ollie's large hand engulfed the boy's and he smiled warmly. He lifted him into his arms. The child did not struggle. Instead he came emotionally unglued and burst into tears on Ollie's shoulder.

Ollie's heart turned over in compassion and he cuddled the boy. He gave the area a last sweep and quickly headed for the beach.

~

"Mayday, mayday, mayday. This is The Dream Catcher."

Jaffa listened to the familiar voice over the radio in the bridge and responded immediately. "Dream Catcher, this is HMAS Hartfield. How may we assist you?"

Joshua moved to the radio operator's side with concern etched into his brow. Wilko also moved away from his station, looking worried.

"Glad to hear your voice Jaff. My first mate and I did a reconnaissance on Finlay Island and found more refugees. They're all dead save a woman and her son. The boy is fine but his mother is sick. I think it's poisoning. It's my guess they may have eaten the same toxic berries that killed the other family we picked up last week."

"Copy that, Ollie. Where are you now?" Jaffa's pencil was ready to jot coordinates.

"Just leaving Finlay on a direct heading to Cairns. Jaff, the woman is severely dehydrated and might not even make it back. Is there any chance of a medevac?"

Jaffa glanced questioningly at the CO.

"Tell him to head for port and we'll get back to him," Joshua instructed.

Jaffa repeated the instruction.

"Roger that. Over." Static followed Ollie's acknowledgement.

"Jaffa, get on the satellite phone and see what can be done about a medevac." Joshua turned to the navigator. "Shep, plot a course to rendezvous with The Dream Catcher. We're only an hour or so from Finlay Island, and The Hartfield is better equipped for a medical emergency than Ollie's boat. On the off chance a medevac can't be arranged, we're it."

Shep moved to the chart table. "Yes sir." With a marker and ruler, he went to work. In moments he had coordinates for the helmsman, who altered their course.

~

"How is she doing?" Farmer stepped from a RHIB onto the fishing charter with the first aid pack slung over one shoulder.

"Not good. She's barely conscious and clearly in pain." Ollie led him inside immediately and their conversation faded into the distance.

As second medic, Jamie followed carrying the foldable stretcher. Coz remained in the RHIB and Amelia trailed the men. She entered the galley and understood why she had been brought along. The men went into the next room, which Amelia guessed was the boat's sleeping quarters.

Against the wall below a port hole was a fixed table. Sitting at the table was a small, frightened dark skinned boy. His wide-eyed gaze was locked on the open door where the men had just gone. Amelia crouched beside him and he turned anxious eyes on her. She smiled kindly and wondered if he spoke English. She decided to try anyway.

"We have come to help." Her voice was calm and gentle.

His gaze swung to the doorway. Not a moment later Jamie and Farmer emerged carrying the child's mother on a stretcher. Ollie and Dayne trailed behind. They walked straight through to the deck.

Amelia wordlessly held out her hand and smiled. The boy slid down from his seat and took it. She led him out to where the ill woman was being transferred onto the RHIB.

"I wish a medevac had been possible." Farmer stepped into the inflatable. "She's in pretty bad shape."

"Just do what you can. And thanks," Ollie replied

gratefully.

Farmer turned his attention to his patient and Coz started the engine. The RHIB bobbed upon the swells and it's motor burbled. Amelia led the boy to the rear of the charter. The child's frightened gaze went from the RHIB to the navy boat floating sixty metres away and he froze.

Ollie lifted him into his arms and pointed to the navy ship. "Good boat. Good people."

Amelia took the opportunity to climb into the RHIB while Ollie went on to explain in simple terms that they were here to help his mum. He moved to pass him to Amelia and the child started to scream. He clutched Ollie's t-shirt with both hands. Clearly Ollie had become his security in a shattered world.

It took both Ollie and Dayne to disentangle his fingers and pass him to Amelia. She held the little guy tightly as he struggled and quickly found a seat. Coz steered the boat toward The Hartfield and the boy's wailing competed with the deep noise of the engine.

Amelia spoke soothing phrases next to his ear, the first words that came to mind. Psalm after psalm dropped from her lips. The boy calmed with the gentle cadence of her voice and he ceased struggling. He wrapped his arms around her neck and held on for all he was worth.

Once the RHIB was hoisted from the water and at deck level, she carried him from the busy quarter deck to the junior sailor's mess. He was still crying when she slid onto a bench seat. He refused to let go his death-grip.

Not knowing how else to comfort him, she rubbed his back and began to softly sing her favourite hymn. The crying stopped, so she kept singing. His breathing evened out and he began to relax. She sang as many songs from church and her childhood as she could recall.

After her memory was exhausted, she smiled to see that he had fallen asleep. She shifted to get comfortable and simply held him close.

Unbeknownst to Amelia, the sweet sound of her voice carried throughout the passageways. Enchanted crew members paused on their way past to listen.

18

"Jackie, she smiled at me!" Linc called over his shoulder.

He was playing with Yasmin on a rug at home. He put his face close to the baby's and made the same silly expression. The corner of her mouth moved upward for a split second and she made an adorable "goo" sound. He grinned. He had always thought babies were boring because they couldn't do much. He was finding out how much fun she really was.

"Are you sure it's not just wind? She shouldn't be able to smile for a few more weeks at least." Jaclyn made her way into the newly furnished nursery.

She peered over her brother's shoulder as he spoke to the infant in exaggerated happy tones. She could not resist a smile of her own. She had clearly never seen him behave ridiculously to amuse a child before, and the change in him must have struck her. He had to admit that he had taken to fatherhood like a duck to water.

"She's going to miss you when you go back to work."

Linc sighed. "A week was all they could manage. It was lucky Lieutenant Yates was available at all."

"I know." Jaclyn allowed the baby to clasp her index

finger in her tiny hand.

"Can I see what you've done?"

Jaclyn looked pleased with her day's work. "Sure."

She led him to the spare room that had previously been a storage facility for his junk. He entered the bedroom that was to be his sister's and was stunned. Just like Yasmin's, she had transformed it.

A single bed sat against one wall and a rosewood dresser occupied the corner. A cheval mirror stood in the opposite corner, and in front of the window overlooking the ocean was Linc's heavy-set antique desk. Her laptop and his printer had been set up on its surface, ready for work. The built-in wardrobe had been cleared and now awaited the arrival of her things from Western Australia. Her housemate was boxing them for her.

"You've done a great job!" He had avoided this room like the plague because of the magnitude of what needed doing. In one day, Jaclyn had made it not only liveable, but attractive too.

He turned to her and was overwhelmed once again by the enormity of the sacrifice she was making.

"Thank you."

She held his gaze and seemed to understand the depth of what he was really communicating. She smiled and reached for her niece. "Anytime."

He willingly handed Yasmin to her. His heart warmed with the love she so obviously felt for his daughter. In that moment, he knew with absolute clarity that everything was going to work out beautifully.

~

Ollie and Dayne waited until the federal police arrived and escorted them to the makeshift camp on Finlay Island. It was difficult facing the tragedy that had occurred there, knowing it didn't have to end that way. Dayne had begun to exhibit signs of stress. Ollie supposed his past was rearing its ugly head.

As they sailed for home that evening, he informed Dayne in no uncertain terms that they were taking the next few weeks off. His friend was the last person on the face of the earth to argue.

~

Nethania used Padi's knife to carve a sixth mark on a large evergreen along the shoreline. She had been marooned for six days, and yet strangely enough, she felt no distress.

She stood at the edge of the forest and watched as dusk painted the sky in warm vibrant colours. The ocean was its mirror, amplifying God's artwork. It caused her heart to sing with delight. She had forgotten the joy of being still and gazing into the face of God. His words resounded in her innermost being more clearly than ever before and they nourished her soul. It was odd, but she felt as though she had finally come home.

~

"Thanks for what you did today with the boy, Teddy." Farmer appeared at Amelia's side in the dinner queue outside the galley.

Amelia frowned in bewilderment. He was clearly directing his remark to her. She concluded it had been a long day and graciously overlooked his slip of the tongue. "My pleasure. How is his mum?"

"I contacted the hospital half an hour ago. She's stable for now. A translator will be brought in to talk with her soon about what happened."

It was Amelia's turn at the serving counter. The chef, Able Seaman Thomas Smith, passed her a plate of lasagne with side salad. She guessed the man to be in his late thirties. He had an amiable smile which was always ready to be shared. She liked him.

She smiled in return. "This looks amazing."

"Thanks Teddy."

Amelia paused with her meal in hand and stared at him strangely. Thomas moved to serve Farmer. However, she remained in place.

Teddy?

The smell of the lasagne and her growling stomach overrode her puzzlement with her shipmates strange behaviour.

She moved to the junior sailor's mess.

Jamie shuffled over on the bench to make room. "Have a seat, Teddy." He directed his attention to the conversation around the full table.

Amelia sat down hard and her plate clattered loudly on the table. An irritated frown puckered her brow. The dinner plate falling the last inch onto the table drew the conversation about fishing tales to a halt and silence fell. Curious and also amused expressions alike regarded her.

"Alright," she demanded in a no nonsense tone, "what's the gag?"

Coz spooned a mouthful of lasagne into his smiling mouth. His eyes gleamed with mischief. "What gag?"

Switch and Ron exchanged grins. Amelia's suspicious gaze passed over the other five cheeky sailors.

"Why is everyone calling me Teddy all of a sudden?" Her scrutiny finally landed upon Jamie beside her.

His brown eyes sparkled with amusement and a smile played about his lips. Faded freckles dotted his loveable face. Amelia fought back the urge to laugh. She sensed their mischief. She also knew it carried no malice.

"Come on Jamie, out with it."

The group watching the interchange looked to be thoroughly enjoying themselves. Amelia knew she was exceedingly shy, and judging by their faces, they were enjoying the feisty side of her personality.

Jamie shrugged and his eyes gleamed with teasing. "You're cute Jonesy. Just like a teddy bear."

Amelia's jaw dropped incredulously and her cheeks

flamed red.

"Especially when you blush," Tyson added wickedly and speared his salad with a fork.

Chuckles broke out around the table. Amelia sent a glare his way. He grinned unrepentantly around a mouthful.

Amelia gave in to the laughter she felt. Mirth rolled around the table in a good natured wave. She finally sighed in resignation. "What am I going to do with you guys?"

Coz winked at her. "Grin and *bear* it, I suppose."

Switch clipped him over the ear. "You're just hilarious."

Her dry tone brought forth a few chuckles and banter continued throughout the meal. Amelia relaxed and settled into her new environment. She silently thanked God for the wonderful people He had placed her amongst.

19

"Alright Tommo, that should just about do it," Amelia stated and fitted the protective meshing back into place.

The chef flicked the switch for the exhaust fan above the cooking area and smiled with pleasure as it went into action. "Thanks Teddy. Wilko is right, you've got magic fingers." He grinned at her.

Amelia just shook her head.

"Hey, are you trying to do me out of a job?" Switch teased as she stepped into the galley. She came close to inspect the exhaust fan and smiled much the way Tommo had. "Not bad for a diesel mechanic."

Used to being ribbed, Amelia simply smiled and took it graciously. "Can I help you prepare lunch?"

Tommo's eyebrows shot upward in surprise. Amelia supposed the galley must be the last place the sailors on board wanted to volunteer. "Sure. That would be great."

Amelia nodded in satisfaction and packed away her tools. "I'll just wash up."

Obviously not wanting to be roped into service as well, Switch made a hasty retreat. "I'd better get onto that faulty socket in the wardroom."

Amelia smiled to herself in amusement and washed

at the sink.

~

"What happens to the boy and his mother now?" Farmer inquired.

Joshua was glad the woman they had rescued was recovering, but also sad she and her son had lost so much in their search for a better life. "They will be taken to a detention centre for processing."

Sitting around the table in the ship's office for a briefing was Shep, Wilko, Lon and Linc, who had recently rejoined them after a week's leave.

Joshua wasn't so sure it had been enough time for his executive officer to regroup, although he could not deny that his friend was coping better. He attributed it to Linc's life changing encounter with God. All the same, he determined to keep a watchful eye out for the lieutenant's welfare.

"Were translators able to establish what happened?" Lon asked next.

A displeased scowl covered Joshua's face. "A little. Apparently her husband arranged passage aboard an Australian yacht for a considerable sum of money. She didn't know the details and couldn't even give the yacht's name or its owner. The other refugees Ollie found were part of the same group being smuggled. She said they were kept in the cargo hold the whole time and only ever had contact with one man, presumably a deck hand."

Wilko looked perplexed. "Then how did they end up on Finlay Island?"

"The scoundrel probably never intended to take them to Australia and dumped them where he thought they couldn't get him in any trouble. He ended up rolling in money and they were off his hands," Shep deduced.

"Close."

Five pairs of eyes regarded the captain curiously as they waited for an answer to something they had clearly puzzled over for days.

"The woman said they were herded onto the island without any explanation and the boat sailed away. Being hungry, they ate what they could find, which was mainly berries. Unfortunately they became gravely ill, all except for the boy who had been seasick and refused to eat a thing. One family tried to escape by raft. As you know, Ollie and Dayne picked them up. The crewmember they had dealt with returned a day or so later, saw they were all sick and simply left them for dead."

"So it's possible they intended to deliver them to the Australian mainland, only a bunch of sick people would have needed medical treatment and therefore would have drawn attention," Linc surmised.

"It seems so." Joshua was disgusted by the despicable way the refugees had been treated.

"But why drop them off on the island in the first place?" Farmer wondered aloud.

Linc put two and two together. "They were afraid they would be nabbed by the navy. Finn Cruickshank knew Macca was suspicious and when the skipper of The Queen Maree escaped, he didn't want to risk getting caught red handed."

"That's what Navcom are thinking at the moment," Joshua filled them in. "It seems our Mr. Cruickshank never docked in his home port after his business voyage to Thailand."

Shep rested his forearms on the table and leant forward with interest. "What does he do other than people smuggling?"

"He's head accountant for a highly lucrative computer company." Joshua took a marker and drew a rough diagram of the Australian coast on the whiteboard mounted on the office wall. He marked in its respective seas. "We're here."

He pointed to the Coral Sea, a couple of hundred kilometres up from Cairns, near Cooktown. "Navcom believes Finn will head back to Thailand, which by now puts him out of Australian waters altogether. We've been tasked to patrol for foreign fishing vessels up the coast toward the Arafura Sea.

"All navy patrol boats will keep a lookout for The Midas, as will P3 Orions, should it re-enter Australian waters. When it does, one of the Armidales will hopefully nab her. Are there any questions?"

The officers seemed satisfied with the captain's explanation and were shortly dismissed. Lunch was being served in the galley, so they headed in that direction.

~

Amelia helped Tommo serve and even carried the crew on the bridge their toasted sandwiches while they were still hot. She noted the absence of the executive officer and wondered if he was alright. Scuttlebutt said he had recently lost someone close. She knew how hard that could be and wished there was something she could do.

She returned to the galley to fetch her own lunch. When the XO failed to make an appearance, she grew worried. She mentioned her concern to the chef and he shook his head.

"You'd mother everyone on this boat if you could." He grinned at her.

Amelia gave him a cheeky smile. "I try."

Tommo chuckled as he wiped down benches. He nodded toward the bain-Maree where the last few ham, cheese and tomato toasted sandwiches were keeping warm. "Farmer said he saw the XO head onto the deck. You can take him those and a brew. He likes his coffee strong and loaded with sugar."

A pleased smile eased away the concern on her features and he appeared relieved to see her happy. Amelia put together a plate and made a strong coffee. She then went in search of the lieutenant.

Linc stood at the quarter deck rail and pondered the direction his life had taken. He wondered what might have happened if Tessa had lived. Could they have patched things up? Would he have still met Jesus?

"Why are things so complicated God?"

"It's called choice."

Linc was stunned by the matter of fact reply and slowly turned. Standing a couple of metres away with a plate of toasted sandwiches in one hand and what smelled like coffee in the other, was a diminutive brunette. Kind hazel eyes regarded him and he relaxed.

In three days he had come to the same conclusion as the crew. Jonesy was a cute bear, and her presence was always a comfort.

"Here sir, you should eat something." She handed him his lunch and the full mug.

Linc looked at the food and then at the tiny woman gently telling him what to do. He was unable to douse a rogue mischievous gleam in his green eyes. "Yes ma'am."

Jonesy caught it and her gaze dropped. Linc watched as her cheeks warmed in embarrassment and he smiled.

Maybe more woman than teddy bear.

He sank onto the deck and leant against the railing. Amelia turned to leave.

"Teddy, what did you mean by choice?"

She stopped and turned side on. Her gaze alighted upon the topaz water churned in the wake of The Hartfield. "I wouldn't spend too much time analysing sir." Her gentle eyes dropped to meet his. "Life becomes complicated because of the choices people make, both good and bad. All impact others in countless ways. The only thing you need to chew over are your own responses. You can only choose for you."

Linc stared at her in stunned silence. She had neatly summed up his situation. His gaze drifted as he pondered the perspective she had offered. He could do nothing about Tessa and the decisions she had made. He could, however, control his own actions. He could be a good father to Yasmin and grow in his new life with God. Where that would take him, he didn't know. He was certain of one thing: as painful as it might be, he had to let Tessa go. Their relationship was a closed book.

Somewhere in his musing, he realised he was alone. Teddy had left as humbly and quietly as she had come.

20

"Come on sir, bowl 'im out!" Jaffa shouted encouragement from behind the wickets.

Linc took a run up and delivered a fast bowl along the sand. Jamie swung the cricket bat and a loud crack resulted. The ball went flying. He and Coz made a dash to swap ends of the pitch twenty paces apart.

Ron fielded the ball and hurled it at the closest set of wickets. Jamie made a last second dive in time to save his skin. The ball toppled the bales at the bowler's end.

Shouts and cheers accompanied the steady roar of the wind and waves. Warm sunshine beat down upon the crew, who were enjoying an afternoon of rest and relaxation on a deserted beach along the northern coastline.

Amelia revelled in white sand between her toes and civilian attire. Her three quarter length jeans and aqua T-shirt, although reserved in comparison with the other women on the crew, suited her perfectly.

Her gaze passed over the thick green shrubbery and low trees hugging the shoreline. Sand as pure as she'd ever seen it stretched for kilometres in both directions. Crystal clear water lapped at the shore.

Urgent shouts brought her attention back to the game. Hands all over the beach were pointing and mouths were yelling. Lon was charging toward her, his intent focus skyward and his hands up to receive a catch. Amelia followed his gaze and spotted the ball falling from the blue expanse. Her heart lurched. She was closer to it than he was.

Without thinking, she trotted backward knee deep into the surf and reached. It dropped the last few metres and her fingers closed around it. An instant later, something cold and wet tackled her mercilessly from behind. She plunged beneath the water. She realised too late it was a breaker as it rolled her along the sandy bottom. Amelia held her breath and forced back a feeling of panic at being completely immersed and out of control.

From out of nowhere, two powerful arms plucked her from the surf and tossed her coughing and spluttering over a shoulder. Lon chuckled and carted her from the sea like a sack of potatoes. Her vision cleared and she regained her senses. Clutched tightly in her hand was the ball and she held it up triumphantly.

"I got it!" Her beaming smile peeked out from behind a curtain of dripping wet hair plastered to her face.

"You're out Coz!" Linc declared.

Laughter broke out around her and Lon set her unceremoniously on her feet.

"Now that's dedication!" the XO said with a grin.

Lon clapped her heartily on the back and she nearly lost her balance. "Way to go Teddy!"

"Sir!" The radio that had previously been clipped to

Jaffa's belt was now in his left hand and his expression was serious.

"What is it Jaff?" Linc turned to the radio operator who was jogging toward him.

"The captain says the radar is picking up a contact. A possible FFV. The captain wants us back on board."

Linc sighed. "Alright guys, you heard the man. Duty calls."

Amelia was swift to obey. There were a few groans. All the same, everyone leapt into action gathering equipment and piling into the two RHIBs partially beached at the edge of the water.

~

The seven metre RHIB pulled alongside a rather old looking fishing boat. Six navy sailors climbed over its railing like agile spider monkeys, armed and in Kevlar vests. Linc was the first aboard.

Three Asian men were waiting curiously on the main deck and offered no resistance. The skipper had obeyed The Hartfield's warning to heave to and pre-pare to be boarded. As a result, weapons remained holstered.

"Who is the master of this vessel?" Linc asked in a clear commanding voice.

The first gentleman stepped forward. He appeared to be in his forties. His long shaggy black hair was drawn back from dark cautious eyes. His skin was almost as weathered as his clothing, and his feet were bare. He smelled as rank as the boat and Linc forced himself to breathe through his mouth rather than his nose.

He assessed the other two with a quick glance. Both were well groomed and contrasted the skipper. Each wore a pair of sandals with their casual attire and baseball caps. Their facial features and short stocky builds were similar. The older of the two had to be in his late fifties. He had time worn features and a smattering of grey throughout his hair. Linc guessed the younger, who was most likely his son, to be in his thirties. He seemed fascinated by the men in uniform, while his father's eyes were veiled and his face unreadable.

"Are you aware you're in Australian waters?" Linc proceeded calmly.

"Yes." The older man's accent was thick. "We go diving."

"Have you done any fishing while in Australian waters?"

"No fish. We dive." The skipper was the one to answer, and his reply was somewhat testy.

Linc noticed Lon smiling to himself. The skipper knew the drill. Illegal fishing meant confiscation of his vessel and jail time.

"May we see your passports?"

"Yes. We have passport. We dive for World War Two Japanese ship," the older man answered, looking relieved. He bowed slightly and disappeared into the wheelhouse.

The younger man admired The Hartfield off the bow, while the skipper studied them shrewdly. The older man returned carrying two passports and handed them to Linc, who then flipped through them. He was happy with what he found.

"Mr. Aiji," he spoke to the older gentleman, "everything seems to be in order. We're required to do a search of the vessel, but if you are truly here to explore old wreckages, and not to capture or remove Australian marine life, then that shouldn't be an issue."

He gestured for his men behind him to go ahead with the search. The skipper did not look pleased, however he did cooperate.

"We'll be off your vessel shortly and you'll be free to go on your way." He hoped that would indeed be the case.

~

"Looking for Japanese World War Two wreckages?" A half smile tugged at Joshua's lips.

Linc was divested of his boarding gear and standing on the bridge behind the navigator's station. "Yes sir."

Joshua resettled in his seat. "That's a new one to add to the books."

Linc watched the foreign vessel depart. "There are a few of them. I've been diving in several wrecks along the east coast, one of them from World War Two."

"And we gave up a perfectly good beach cricket

match for a bunch of tourists!" Jaffa muttered several feet away at the radio desk.

Joshua and Linc exchanged amused glances and Shep grinned without sympathy.

21

Amelia strode purposefully to the wardroom. Wilko had invited her to the Bible study that met regularly each week while the crew was at sea. He had said everyone was welcome.

Her steps faltered. She hesitated a metre from the wardroom and listened to the men inside. It didn't escape her notice that every voice drifting through the open doorway was male. She recognised each one and realised all were officers, save for Coz.

Amelia glanced at her watch. She was on time. Judging by the easy going dialogue inside, they hadn't started yet.

"You look as nervous as I feel."

Amelia jerked with fright and spun around. One hand held her Bible and the other flew to her chest in surprise.

Lieutenant Hobbs' eyes took on an amused gleam. "You look like you just got caught sneaking in past curfew."

Amelia released the breath she was holding and grinned. She was grateful that all of the crew's constant ribbing had cured her of blushing.

Her smile faded and her answer was direct. "Wilko said I'd be welcome, but the group in there are all guys.

145

I'm worried my presence will hinder their freedom to share."

"I wouldn't know Teddy. This is my first study too. I don't even own a Bible."

For the first time Amelia could recall, the XO looked uncertain and vulnerable. She sympathised. She offered a kind smile and gave his arm a reassuring squeeze. She turned, drew a fortifying breath and stepped into the wardroom.

~

Linc was taken aback. He had witnessed Jonesy's compassion with the crew on a daily basis, but had never had her caring so openly directed toward him. He found his heart hungering for more. The emotion surprised him. He hadn't felt that way since Tessa had left nearly six months ago.

"Are you coming or not sir? They're not so bad after all," Jonesy's cheeky voice called.

Male laughter floated out into the hallway. Linc smiled and entered. He glanced at the small mechanic beside Wilko. Her eyes sparkled wickedly. He wondered how a person could encapsulate such shyness and mischief at one time. He did not have time to ponder the question as he was welcomed and quickly absorbed into the group.

~

Linc entered his berth a week later after a long, but productive day. The captain had granted a day of liberty in Cape Town. Linc would rather it have been in Cairns so that he could see Yasmin.

Jaclyn's regular emails included updates, pictures and videos. Linc was grateful for everything she sent.

He sighed and sat at the desk he shared with Shep.

The blue curtain across Shep's rack was pushed aside. Linc glanced at his roommate, surprised he was in bed already.

"You were quiet. I didn't even know you were in here." His eyes went to a notebook in Shep's hands.

"I was reading. This is a good book."

Linc frowned at his friend stretched out in his rack. "It's a spiral notebook."

"Teddy wrote it." His expression was matter-of-fact. "It's about-"

Linc was astonished. "Teddy wrote a book?"

Shep shrugged. "Sure. She's always writing stories." He glanced curiously at Linc. "Haven't you ever wondered what she gets up to while everyone else is relaxing in front of a movie?"

Now that Linc thought about it, Jonesy did tend to cloister herself away every chance she got. He had even seen her with a notebook and pen in hand on occasion.

"That woman never ceases to amaze me."

you are not alone. You've been adopted into His family and now have more brothers and sisters than you'll know what to do with. Remember, you can choose your friends but not your relatives.'

Linc grinned at the cute sketch of a bear beneath her inscription. Next to the bear she had signed it simply, 'Teddy.'

He crossed to the desk and laid his new Bible beside a pad of paper. He sat and composed a letter for Jaclyn. He would type it later and e-mail it when it was his allotted personal computer time.

'Is it possible to love a woman you've known for only two weeks? I've experienced attraction, infatuation, and even love. This is somehow different. It includes all of those things, and also friendship, respect and admiration. She's also seriously cute.

Tess has, in reality, been gone for over five months. Although I loved her, it's been finished for a long time. I guess I just answered my own question.

It's times like these I hate regulations. Pray for me? I don't know what to do.

Give Yasmin a kiss for me?

Love Linc.'

He folded the note and tucked it safely in his pocket. He knew the email he was sending soon would drive his sister to distraction. She would want details he could not give. Even if Teddy wasn't under his command, would she even be interested?

His past played on his mind. Yet for all of the complications it brought to the present, he suspected she was a rare woman who would be able to take it in her stride.

He abruptly strode from the room. It was pointless agonising over a relationship that did not exist. Regulations were regulations and he had learned to live by them, whether he liked them or not.

22

"Sir, a P3 Orion picked up a vessel bearing one-hundred and fifteen degrees latitude, one-hundred and thirty-five degrees longitude," Jaffa alerted the captain.

Joshua rose from his chair and looked over the navigator's shoulder. "Shep, can you pick it up on radar?"

"It's there." He pointed to a moving blip on the screen. "It's signature belongs to The Midas."

A slow grin stole over Joshua's features. "Mr. Cruikshank, you're about to be nabbed." He turned to the radio operator. "Pipe boarding stations." He spoke next to the helmsman. "Adjust our course forty-five degrees, revolutions two zero zero zero."

The bridge came alive. Joshua fixed his determined gaze out the large windshield.

"You picked the wrong day to sail home."

~

"Out of curiosity, why me sir?"

The bosun thrust a bullet proof vest at Amelia in the armoury. Squeezed into the tight space were six other sailors donning flak jackets, radios and side arms.

Lon clapped her encouragingly on the back and her balance teetered. Did he know how strong he was?

"Because Coz is in his rack with the flu, and out of the others I've trained who are not on the boarding party, you're the most capable."

Amelia doubted it.

Farmer grinned sideways at her as he zipped up his vest. "Don't worry Teddy, the sea is like glass today. Just get us on board and stay with the RHIB. We'll do the rest."

Amelia smiled. She was secretly excited to be driving. She had thoroughly enjoyed it during drills.

~

"Vessel on my port bow, stop and heave to. I intend to board you," Jaffa issued the warning over the ship's loud speaker. They failed to respond, just as radio cautions had also gone unheeded.

Joshua keyed the microphone and spoke to his men standing by in the port side RHIB. "Insert, insert, insert." He waited with baited breath as the inflatable sped away from The Hartfield.

It nudged the yacht's stern and six navy personnel boarded in quick succession. Linc was in the lead. The radio on the bridge crackled to life not five minutes later.

"Sir, the skipper's armed and Jamie's down. Repeat, we have a man down."

~

Amelia's eyes widened at the sound of gunfire inside the yacht. She recognised Linc's authoritative voice yelling a warning. She was not prepared for the wild man who leapt from the balcony onto the main deck. He landed on his feet and rolled, coming up on one knee to fire at Linc above him.

The executive officer ducked to avoid the bullets flying his way. Meanwhile the gunman made a dash for the RHIB floating at the stern. He scaled the yacht rail and his crazed eyes locked on Amelia. She drew her weapon.

Behind him, men came charging through the salon and Linc jumped from the balcony in hot pursuit. However, the madman was bent on escape. As he stepped into the RHIB, he aimed and fired. Amelia pulled the trigger point blank at the same time.

She heard her assailant cry out simultaneously as something ripped into her with the force of a Mack truck. It knocked her off her feet and slammed her against the rollbar. Blinding pain flooded her senses. She landed with her back against the inflated rim and her legs stretched before her.

Sprawled on the floor on his side at her feet, the gunman groaned and clutched his chest. He suddenly became very still.

Amelia was horrified. "Father forgive me? Oh God,

please forgive me?"

She became acutely aware she was clutching something metallic. She raised it off the floor, saw that it was her handgun, and tossed it across the boat. She had used her nine millimetre for the first time and killed a man.

~

Linc leapt the yacht rail and stepped onto the RHIB. He removed the pistol from the skipper's limp hand and felt for a pulse in his neck. He glanced up at Amelia, his expression unreadable, and noted tears tracking down her cheeks. He heard her pleas for forgiveness and his heart broke. It had all gone so terribly wrong.

She was only supposed to mind the RHIB, not be forced to shoot the crazy man who panicked when he spotted the navy.

"Teddy, are you hurt?" He stepped over the body and knelt in front of her.

Her horrified gaze was locked on Gareth Utano and her face had drained of all colour. "Sir, I've killed him. I think I've killed him." She choked on a sob.

Linc took her face between his hands and forced her to look at him. "Were you hit when he fired?"

She seemed to notice him for the first time. "Yes."

Linc felt the whispered word like a blow to the stomach. Lon and Tyso barrelled onto the scene. Tyso waited anxiously on the deck while Lon climbed into the inflatable and repeated Linc's check for a pulse.

"He's dead."

"Are you sure?" Large wounded hazel eyes regarded him from an ashen face.

Lon's look was regretful. "I'm sure."

Amelia's face crumpled in misery and she wept. Linc checked her flak jacket for a hole. He found one below her ribs on her right side. With a growing sense of dread, he undid her vest.

Lon looked on apprehensively. "Is she alright?"

"How's Jamie?"

"Farmer is bringing him up. His jacket caught the round."

Linc sucked in a breath as the vest pulled aside to reveal blood soaking through two layers of clothing. He heard Lon behind him mutter a rare expletive. Linc immediately applied pressure with his hand.

Amelia cried out and grasped his collar.

He stared into her pain clouded eyes and his heart squeezed in agony. "I'm sorry Teddy."

Lon revved the RHIB engine. "Tys, help Farmer load Jamie, then you and I will assist Woody with the round up of crew. Make it fast!"

Amelia's rapid breathing slowed and her eyes slid shut. Her body went limp, her hand slipped and her head dropped forward. Linc gently laid her on the floor on her side, keeping tight pressure on the gushing wound. He checked for a pulse with his free hand and was reassured to find one, albeit erratic.

"Hurry it up! We're losing her!"

Lon stepped from the RHIB to take over the boarding party. Boots upon polished boards sounded above him and Linc mentally sighed with relief. In minutes they would be back aboard The Hartfield and help would be on the way.

23

A glint of gold caught Padi's eye. He squeezed through the badly buckled doorway into what had once been the captain's cabin.

They had found the wreckage exactly where Dake Kado had said it would be, not far from a grouping of small islands on the Great Barrier Reef. The old World War Two Japanese battleship was at least fifty metres down, and it's severely compromised structure gave evidence to its swift and violent demise. It was no wonder there had been no survivors. The biologist supposed it was for that very reason the treasure had remained untouched all of these years.

Padi's torchlight bounced off gold scattered across the captain's cabin floor that had not lost its lustre. He grinned. At least the finders had written their families of their discovery prior to their deadly encounter with an Australian warship. However, the falling out between the Kado and Aiji families over its recovery and rightful ownership, meant that now time was of the essence.

Padi took the bag tucked in his weight belt and began filling it with the scattered coins. He then removed pieces of rotting furniture and debris. Inbuilt into one wall was what had once been the captain's rack. Beneath it was a steel draw slightly ajar and encrusted with coral.

The ocean's resilience never ceased to amaze him. A shipwreck, which was nothing more than a huge hunk of twisted metal on the sea floor, had been transformed into a haven for fish and a variety of sea life.

Padi swam closer and after several failed efforts, managed to wrench the draw free. He gaped at what was inside. He had no doubt that the reluctant and impatient men on the boat fifty metres above him would finally get up off their lazy backsides and offer assistance.

As Padi ran his gloved hands through the gold and jewels stored safely away beneath the ocean's surface from man's greedy eyes, he knew there would be more than enough to go around.

~

Farmer carried Amelia carefully up the stairs at the stern of The Hartfield, Linc moving with him to keep pressure on the wound with his hand. Joshua, Wilko and Switch were waiting on the quarterdeck with a stretcher for their injured crewmember.

Farmer wordlessly lowered Amelia's limp body onto it. "Keep the pressure on."

Linc obeyed. She had lost too much blood. Wilko and Farmer lifted an end each and Linc walked beside Amelia, his hand pressing firmly against the gushing bullet hole in her stomach. As an efficient team, they took her inside. Jamie followed closely behind them looking worse for wear.

Joshua remained on the quarterdeck at the stern rail. "Switch, Jaffa is on the radio with Navcom trying to arrange a medevac. Transfer the prisoners from the yacht and we'll hold them on the quarterdeck for now. Then I want Lon to lead a steaming party to sail The Midas to port in Cairns. We'll sail on ahead and get Teddy as close to the mainland as we can. It will make a pickup just that bit swifter." Switch climbed down into the RHIB as he spoke.

"Yes sir." She indicated the gunman sprawled behind her. "What do you want us to do with him?"

"I'll help you carry him on board now. I'll have some-one see to him soon." As he spoke, he was striding down the stairs at the back of the ship into the inflat-able. He took the dead man's legs and Switch got a solid grip of his arms. Between the two of them, they toted the body on board.

"Now go!" Joshua demanded, even as Switch scoot-ed back into the boat.

The RHIB's engine roared as she steered toward the yacht drifting nearby. Joshua headed straight for the wardroom to check how his people were doing.

24

"I've got a doctor on hold." Jaffa looped a headset over Farmer's ear while he worked.

"Thanks." Farmer stepped back from the patient and shed his flak jacket.

Jaffa took it and exited the crowded room. Jamie, although likely suffering from cracked ribs, was digging through the wall cabinet for bandages and morphine. Linc was still keeping pressure on Amelia's wound. Space was limited and so Wilko waited in the corridor outside. That was where Joshua found him upon his approach.

"Wilko, I need you to photograph that body and bag it. Take him to the garbage room. It's not ideal, but it will have to do."

Wilko reluctantly nodded. "Yes sir."

Joshua peered inside the wardroom to find it abuzz with activity. Farmer was conversing with a doctor via satellite phone through his headset. Linc was trying to stem the bleeding and Jamie was laying out equipment Farmer would need. Seeing everything as under control as it could be, Joshua headed for the bridge.

With the cache winched from the deep and dumped on the deck, the three fishermen stood back and stared in wonder. It was the mother load of eighteenth century gold and jewels.

Padi surfaced at the rear of the boat and climbed aboard. They did not move or pay him heed. Bruno Dizane's greedy eyes shone with amazement. He had not believed Padi when he described what he was after. It was only idle curiosity and money that led him to hire out his boat. Now he was glad he had. It was theirs. All theirs.

"We sail to Cairns and I call Mr. Kado."

Garvey's shrewd gaze snapped to meet Bruno's and he subtly shook his head. Bruno nodded ever so slightly in return. Both were in agreement. Someone would die before they would split this find. Bruno forced a smile.

"You head below an' clean up. We'll crate this an' set sail."

Padi looked elated and he smiled broadly. He passed trustingly by the three men. He appeared confused when the world suddenly went black and the deck rushed up to greet him.

Bruno, who had dealt the blow, stared down at the unconscious man and then glanced at his silent crew staring at him. Neither of them looked surprised.

"Get 'im below an' tie 'im up."

They grinned at one another.

~

The Hartfield was well underway when Joshua was finally free to drop in on the ship's medic again. When he entered the wardroom, Jamie was sitting on a bench with his shirt removed and Farmer was probing his bruised, and possibly cracked, ribs.

Amelia was still unconscious on her side on the table. Her outer shirt had been removed, and her grey t-shirt cut away below the bust. Her midsection was padded and heavily bandaged.

Linc leaned against the sink in the corner. His eyes were riveted to Amelia's face where freckles stood out against deathly pale skin. Her chest gently rose and fell in a steady rhythm, but Linc did not look comforted.

Joshua stood just inside the door. "How's she doing?"

Farmer glanced over his shoulder gravely. "The same."

By the looks of it, Jamie was lucky the bullet had hit where it did. A few inches lower and the impact might have ruptured organs and caused internal bleeding.

"I take it the bullet hit a seam between the Kevlar pockets in her vest?"

"Unfortunately."

Jamie winced as Farmer wound a bandage tightly around his ribs. Linc abruptly pushed away from the sink and strode from the room. Joshua noted his hasty exit and recognised that grief must be riding him hard. He would check on his friend soon.

First, he moved to Amelia's side and took her right hand. His heart squeezed painfully. In such a short time, she had won over the entire crew with her kind and gentle nature.

"Teddy."

He was surprised when she stirred and increased pressure on his hand. Her eyes opened and she squinted against the fluorescent lighting.

"She's awake." Joshua knelt so that he was eye to eye with the small mechanic.

Farmer left Jamie and stood beside Joshua.

"You're going to be okay. You're back on board The Hartfield and we're steaming for port."

Amelia blinked sleepily. Her gaze grew distant and suddenly she shut her eyes tightly. Joshua recognised a flashback when he saw one. He had experienced them himself a few times before.

"It should have been me," she whispered through parched lips and met his gaze.

"No." He squeezed her hand and released it. "You did what you were trained to do. 'The rod was made for the back of fools.'"

Amelia frowned at him. "Proverbs?"

Joshua smiled. "You know your Bible."

"I never understood what that verse meant." Her words were slurred from painkillers, exhaustion and blood loss.

"It means that punishment was made for those who foolishly break the law. It's our job as navy to enforce Australian law in our waters. Gareth Utano and Finn Cruickshank broke that law when they began people smuggling, and again when Utano tried to kill Jamie to evade arrest. He would have killed every sailor standing between him and freedom. The only thing that could stop a man like that is a bullet.

"It was his choice, Teddy. I just wanted to thank you for putting your life on the line and saving lives today." Joshua knew that had he been in Amelia's shoes, he would not have hesitated.

Her face crumpled and tears slipped down her cheeks. Joshua had a hunch what might comfort her in the midst of this anguish. He began to pray.

"Heavenly Father, please lift this weight of guilt off Teddy's shoulders? Comfort her? Help her to be at peace, and please give her a deep awareness of Your presence? I thank You on behalf of every sailor aboard for sending her to us. She has shone Your light and daily shared Your love. Let it all come back to her now, pressed down, shaken together and running over? In Your Son's name I pray this."

"Amen," two male voices chimed in unison.

Joshua glanced up at Farmer in surprise. The man had tears in his eyes, and Jamie respectfully crossed himself. He returned his focus to Amelia. She smiled wearily, and Joshua could see the visible effect of Christ's peace stealing over her in full measure.

"Thank you," she managed in a whisper.

He smiled kindly. "You hang in there okay?"

She sighed and gave in to exhaustion's irresistible pull. He rose and walked to the door. He paused with a hand on the doorframe.

"A chopper will meet us in fifteen minutes."

Farmer glanced at him distractedly. "Good." He returned his curious stare to the woman sleeping peacefully. Despite her suffering, her countenance had softened and her lips turned gently up at the corners in an expression of contentment.

Farmer appeared stunned, and Joshua thought he could make a good guess as to why. It was difficult to deny the existence of God when He was so visibly at work in someone's life.

25

Linc closed the door to his cabin and sat on the edge of his bunk. His gaze landed upon his hands where Amelia's blood had now dried in the crevices he had been unable to scrub. His shirt and trousers were covered in crimson.

The circumstances surrounding those dark stains troubled him deeply. If only he had been faster! Now Amelia lay slowly dying.

A distant conversation sprang unexpectedly to mind, and Linc could still picture the diminutive brunette regarding him with kind hazel eyes.

"Why are things so complicated God?"

"It's called choice."

Linc had been stunned by the matter of fact reply.

"... What did you mean by choice?"

"I wouldn't spend too much time analysing sir." Her *gentle eyes met his. "Life becomes complicated because of the choices people make, both good and bad. All impact others in countless ways. The only thing you need to chew over are your own responses. You can only choose for you."*

You can only choose for you. The phrase played repeatedly in his thoughts, challenging his new faith.

"Please God, don't let me lose Teddy too?"

You can only choose for you. What choice will you make? The foreign thought nudged his mind.

Linc wanted to shout, to rail, to run. Instead he knelt. "I'll follow You Jesus, even if she dies."

A sense of assurance came on the heels of his decision, and he marvelled at experiencing the same presence as the day he had stood by Tessa's grave. Unseen arms wrapped around him. Still on his knees, he poured out his brokenness before God.

~

"Let's just dump 'im an' take the gold." Trevor shrugged dispassionately.

"An' have 'im talk if some joker finds 'im?" Garvey objected. "Nah, let's just kill 'im an' feed 'im to the sharks."

Bruno leaned back in his seat at the helm. He regarded first Trevor leaning against the door frame with a shoulder and his ankles crossed, and then Garvey on a bench by the window. One leg was drawn onto the bench and bent at the knee, the other stretched out in front of him. His hands were looped behind his head.

They looked for all the world like they were discussing the catch of the day, not disposing of their passenger.

Bruno decided for them. "For now let's just offload the loot and hide it on Murphy Island."

"What?"

"There's no way we're gunna leave-"

Bruno held up his hand for quiet. His expression was fierce. Both men fell silent. They had learned from experience not to cross him.

"We can't very well sail into port loaded with gold to report a man missing."

Trevor and Garvey exchanged sly smiles.

~

Joshua knocked. "Linc?"

"Yes sir."

At the muffled reply, Joshua opened the door and stepped into his executive officer's berth. The room was empty, however the bathroom door was ajar. He noted a pile of clothing on the floor with obvious blood stains. It was a stark reminder of the day's terrible events.

"Are you alright?" He moved further into the room.

Through the gap between the bathroom door and the frame, he saw Linc with a towel about his waist, wet hair in tight curls, scrubbing his hands at the sink.

"I can't get it off."

Alarm bells rang loudly in Joshua's mind at the edge of panic in his friend's voice and he opened the door fully. With the way the younger man was attacking his fingers with a scrub brush, it was a wonder there was any skin left.

He placed a reassuring hand on Linc's shoulder and

gave it a squeeze. "She's going to be okay."

The traumatised executive officer scrubbed harder at the blood beneath his nails. "You don't know that."

Joshua removed his hand. "Until I'm told otherwise, that's what I'm choosing to believe."

Linc stopped scrubbing and tossed the brush in the sink in frustration. He stepped away and leaned against the wall, hands by his sides and his head tipping back in defeat. "It's my fault."

Joshua regarded him carefully and decided a firm and direct approach was best. "I'm going to tell you the exact same thing I've been telling every other sailor on this boat feeling bad about what happened."

Linc met his gaze.

"Someone was going to end up in the wardroom today wounded no matter what any of us did. Nothing short of shooting Utano on the spot could have stopped it. It wouldn't have mattered who was driving that RHIB. They all would have been a target and they all would have done what Jonesy did."

"A selfish part of me wishes it was someone else. Then I feel guilty, because who would I choose to take her place? No one but myself," he concluded in an anguished whisper.

"I understand the logic, but it won't help."

Linc sighed and ran a hand through his hair. "I know."

"Get dressed, Lieutenant," Joshua ordered in a gentle tone. "We need to talk."

Linc nodded resignedly. "I'm sorry sir. I should still be on duty."

"Lon is heading the steaming party, and things here are under control." In fact, Joshua was grateful Linc had ended up back on board. That he was suffering post traumatic stress was more than obvious. The day's events were sure to have also set him back in the grieving process.

Joshua left Linc with instructions to meet him in the ship's office for a debriefing. After that, he planned to have a private discussion about his friend taking some more time off.

26

"Is it done?" Bruno asked coldly from his place at the helm.

Garvey dropped onto the bench he had occupied earlier looking satisfied. Trevor appeared in the doorway of the wheelhouse. His expression and pale features gave Bruno his answer.

"He sunk like a stone. Poor blighter won't be talkin' where he's goin'."

The corner of Bruno's mouth lifted in a mirthless smile. He returned his gaze to the sea stretching before them. In the distance, three islands rose from the ocean clothed in dark green jungle.

"Good. We'll stash the loot an' head for port."

Mention of the gold must have lifted Trevor's mood, for he was able to pass Garvey a grin.

~

Unable to sleep late that night, Linc checked his email. He opened his inbox and saw that Jaclyn had replied. Feeling desperate for some kind of comfort, he clicked on his sister's email and began to read.

'I'm so excited for you, Linc. I know it seems soon to be considering a relationship after Tessa's death, but I must confess your news is an answer to prayer.

I have been asking God for a wife for you. You need a woman to love and who will love you; someone in whom you trust and can have a good friendship. You need someone who will support you and Yasmin and who understands the demands of your job. One question: does she share your faith?'

Linc stopped reading. A madman's bullet had destroyed any hope he had harboured. A helicopter had airlifted Amelia to the mainland. However, prior to that she had slipped from consciousness and could not be roused. Her vital signs had been sketchy at best. Linc was no fool. Her chances of survival were slim. That reality left a gaping hole in his heart; one he knew he would never be able to fill.

~

Amelia opened heavy lids and stared at a white ceiling in confusion. Her foggy senses detected a steady beep to her left. Voices and footsteps drifted in from further away, and the smell of disinfectant reached her nostrils.

Hospital. She had made it. Her extremities felt numb and a moment of panic hit her. Movement to her right drew her attention and she rolled her head slowly in that direction.

"Amelia?"

She smiled wearily at the familiar voice. "Carrie." Her eyes drifted shut of their own volition. She willed them open. "What are you doing here?"

Carrie Lonigan smiled compassionately. "Lon told me what happened. I came as soon as I heard."

All Amelia could recall was the wardroom and the captain praying for her. "What day is it?"

"Tuesday. You were airlifted from The Hartfield yesterday afternoon and spent the evening in surgery."

Carrie leaned forward in her chair and Amelia was able to look into her face without effort.

"They were able to remove the bullet and repair the damage."

The news was a huge relief, but still worry nagged at the back of her mind. "Then why can't I feel my hands and feet?"

Carrie smiled in understanding. "Don't worry. That's just the high dosage of painkillers. They'll ease it back in a day or so."

Amelia relaxed and sent a grateful prayer winging toward heaven. She remembered her shipmates and her heart squeezed painfully. "The crew... Do they know I'm okay?" Her words were slurred by fatigue and drugs.

"Just rest, Amelia. Josh Donnelly has been in touch

with the hospital. The Hartfield docks in an hour and I'm sure you'll have a host of visitors."

Amelia could no longer fight the fatigue pulling her under. A small smile touched her lips as her eyes drifted shut. "My family?"

"They've been notified."

~

Carrie watched her friend drift off and shifted in her chair to get comfortable. What she hadn't had a chance to say, was that Joshua himself had contacted Amelia's family after the navy's official notification.

Victoria was a long way away, and from what Joshua had shared, Amelia's parents did not have the money or health to travel that distance. Neither would Amelia make it home immediately after being discharged from hospital. She would need quite a few weeks before being cleared to travel. Even then there would be many more months of rest and recuperation. She had a long road ahead of her.

Carrie had not yet discussed her plan with her husband, however she had no concern that he would object. As she watched her friend sleep, she was already plotting how she would rearrange things at home.

Like every other woman married to a sailor, shifting towns and even states was a way of life. One's friends tended to become one's family, and Amelia was no different.

The woman didn't know it yet, but she was about to be absorbed into their community as one of their own.

~

Linc stood in the doorway to Amelia's room and released a shaky breath. She was asleep, but very much alive.

In the chair beside her bed was an enormous brown bear with cream paws and nose. It was at least half the size of its new owner and wore a huge red ribbon.

Linc smiled. The crew had obviously been to visit. He moved silently into the room and took a second chair from against the far wall where there was an empty bed. He sat on her left, opposite the bear and worked to process the events of the last forty-eight hours.

He rested his elbows on his knees and his chin on his fists. His gaze lingered on Amelia's pale features smoothed peacefully in sleep. It was true that beauty was in the eye of the beholder. He loved her freckles and the colour of her eyes, especially when they lit with mischief. He loved the way her hair escaped her ponytail in cute curly wisps around her face.

A memory of her dripping wet and triumphantly holding a ball sprang to mind and he smiled. He didn't know how it was possible to love her after such a short time, but it had happened. Linc recalled his sister's email and supposed it had something to do with her prayers.

Amelia stirred and opened her eyes.

"Hey sailor," he greeted softly.

Her head rolled on the pillow and she met his gaze. She smiled and her eyes closed of their own will. "I wondered how you were doing, sir." Her speech was still affected by exhaustion.

Linc gently brushed strands of brown hair from her face. "You don't have to 'sir' me here, Teddy."

Her sleepy eyes opened and regarded him with a warm twinkle. He realised it was rare that she had seen him in civilian attire. He was wearing jeans and a trendy orange t-shirt, with thongs on his feet. A far cry from navy uniform.

For the first time he could recall, she let her guard down and seemed to simply be appreciating the sight of him. He knew his hair was wind tussled and he looked tanned from hours in the sun. His green eyes however, were troubled.

"Are you okay?" she asked.

"I'm worried about you."

Amelia read more than he was willing to say. "It wasn't your fault."

He studied her carefully and felt emotion choke him when tears filled her eyes.

"I'm sorry, Linc. I let you down and now everyone is feeling bad."

He frowned. "Where did that train of logic come from? You did what any one of us would have done."

She stared at him in misery. "But not fast enough. If I'd been quicker, I might not have been hit."

Linc's eyes took on a steely glint. "Don't go second guessing yourself."

"Yes sir."

Linc noted her immediate response as a junior sailor to his authority and was irritated, more at himself than at her. "Don't you go 'siring' me either Teddy Jones."

An angry challenge sparked in her hazel eyes. "Or what?"

Linc leaned back in his chair and smiled in amusement. At least she hadn't lost her pluck. He resisted a chuckle when she scowled at him.

"I'll do you a deal, Teddy," he began soberly.

She assessed him warily. "What kind of deal?"

"I won't blame myself if you won't."

Amelia's fire drained. Linc watched turmoil darken her gaze and knew he had asked something tremendously big. Her sensitive nature was taking on more responsibility than it should. Something he had read in his new Bible that morning dropped into his thoughts.

"Who is condemning you, Teddy? It certainly isn't God. Even if killing Gareth Utano was wrong, and I don't believe it was, I heard you telling God you were sorry. Is the blood of Christ shed in your place insufficient to forgive?"

Amelia stared at him in stunned silence. He was aware she knew her Bible well, and probably could recite the verses in Romans eight and one John one, from which he had drawn his challenge.

"I can't forgive myself."

At her quiet admission, Linc leaned forward and took

her hand. His gaze radiated loving truthfulness. "And we both know that's pride."

She swallowed hard and blinked back tears. "You're right." She shifted her focus to the ceiling.

Had he said too much? Linc gave her hand a squeeze. "Are you alright?"

Amelia rolled her head on the pillow again to look at him. She offered him a reassuring smile. "I'm fine. I just need to think on what you've said."

Linc smiled in return, although it did not quite reach his eyes. He berated his timing. It was past nine in the evening and she was already exhausted. "I'd better go." He gave her hand another squeeze and released it.

"Thanks for coming."

He could see her tongue was itching to add 'sir', and he restrained a smile. "My pleasure."

Her watchful gaze followed him to the door. "Sir?"

Linc turned and raised one brow in challenge. Amelia smiled shyly.

"Linc."

His eyes glimmered with humour. "Yes Teddy."

"Will you come again?"

He looked into her shy, hopeful face and under-stood what that request had cost her. He grinned and winked.

"Try and stop me."

Amelia sighed with satisfaction and closed her eyes. Sleep was obviously never far away, and it appeared to be crowding in quickly. Linc quietly exited and headed for home.

Paperwork had detained him when the rest of the crew had been dismissed. He hadn't even seen Yasmin or his sister. All the same, he was reluctant to leave Amelia. The knowledge he had the next two weeks off and could visit her every day if he wished, made his departure a little easier.

27

"Have you got that patch of his wetsuit?" Bruno switched off the engine and turned to Garvey.

His friend was coming up from the galley. "I'll fetch it."

Through the windshield, Bruno watched Trevor moor the boat to the jetty. It was time to enact part two of their plan. Garvey came back into the wheelhouse from the outer deck with a bloodied scrap of material. It had been stashed in the tackle box.

Bruno studied it carefully. The bull shark they had caught had done a terrific job of tearing it to shreds. "Is the blood his? You know the cops will check."

"Do you think I'm stupid? Of course it's his. That knock to 'is head gushed like a river. I soaked the wet-suit in it 'fore we tossed 'im overboard. Then with the shark and that mayday call... Don't worry boss. They'll buy our story."

Bruno's gaze travelled out the window to where two police officers got out of their car at the end of the jetty. "Let's hope so, 'cos 'ere they come."

Garvey followed Bruno's line of sight. "Leave it with me. I got it covered."

Bruno clapped his first mate confidently on the back. "They're all yours."

~

Amelia heard movement and turned toward the sound. She spotted Linc in the doorway and her heart skipped a beat. He had said he would come again, but she had not allowed herself to believe that he actually would. He looked wonderful in a pair of red shorts, and a white t-shirt. Although it was loose, it was unable to hide a strapping physique.

She was so used to seeing him impeccably groomed, that the day old stubble on his chin was a delightful surprise.

She berated herself for her schoolgirl crush, but had to admit that somehow it had been moving past that stage in the last week alone. There was something special about Lincoln Hobbs, and it was more than just his rugged good looks. The eyes watching her were filled with care and a little anxiety.

Amelia smiled in welcome and shyly tugged the sheet a little higher, suddenly very aware that she looked a mess.

Linc beamed and strode casually to the spare chair beside her bed. "You must be feeling better if they've got you sitting up today."

Her smile was lopsided. "Worse, they made me walk to the bathroom. My blood pressure dropped so low I thought I was going to pass out." She had expected him to chuckle, however concern darkened his green eyes.

"How are you feeling now?"

She shelved her surprise and smiled reassuringly. "I'm fine, really. Just sore and very tired. How about you?" Her gentle gaze probed his, looking for an accurate answer.

They stared at one another and his gaze softened. "You're in hospital and you're still trying to look after others."

"Not everyone," she whispered. Her shocked gaze held his. She hadn't intended to say that aloud.

A slow smile stole over his face and hers flamed red. She studied the covers intently in the silence that followed. When she dared venture a glance at her executive officer, she found him watching her with an odd hesitance in his usually warm eyes, almost as though he were weighing his next words.

Amelia chastised herself and decided to beat him to the punch. "I'm sorry, sir. That was inappropriate."

"I told you, Teddy, don't 'sir' me when we're not on duty. And don't apologise. I think any man would be privileged to be cared for by you."

Amelia could not bring herself to look at him. He knew. He knew she had feelings for him. How humiliating! The last thing she wanted was his pity. She had always known she didn't stand a chance with anyone; she was too plain and ordinary to draw attention from the opposite sex, let alone someone of Linc's calibre.

"Especially me," he added softly.

Amelia's gaze lifted and she stared at the man beside her. Had she heard correctly? "Pardon?"

"I said any man would be privileged to be cared for by you, especially me."

Amelia searched his face for some sign that he was joking or that this was another prank by her fun loving crew. But no, sincerity shone from his open expression, and a good measure of vulnerability. He was serious.

"What are you saying?"

Linc dropped his eyes to the fingers in his lap. "Teddy, I want you to shoot straight with me." He cringed. "Sorry for the bad pun."

It was true that the trauma of what had happened would likely stay with her for a very long time. Yet she understood that Linc was just as affected by it as she was. They were walking the same road in a way.

He took another breath and seemed to draw courage. "I'm going to be direct with you, and I want you to do the same with me."

"Okay." She frowned in puzzlement. What was on his mind that he found hard to express?

"I don't know what you want to do career-wise after all of this." He indicated the machinery surrounding her bed. "I just know that I'd like to see you. If I have to transfer off the ship so we're not under the same command, I will."

Amelia was stunned speechless. She stared at him in amazement for several silent minutes. Finally he shifted uncomfortably and scratched his lightly whiskered chin.

"Teddy, say something. You're unnerving me."

Amelia swallowed. "You want to date me?"

183

Shep smiled. "Oh, she asked me to pass something on to you. Said it was basic navy provisions, or something like that. I left it on your rack." He went straight back to reading Teddy's story.

Intrigued, Linc moved to his bunk. Sure enough, there was a small rectangular package on his pillow. He sat on the edge of his mattress and opened it with great curiosity. The brown paper fell away to reveal a leather bound New King James Bible.

Emotion choked him and he swallowed hard in an effort to maintain control. Joshua had loaned him a copy during the week, but it wasn't the same as having one of his own that he could mark and scribe notes in the margins.

He turned the book over in his hands and admired the gilded edged pages. He could not resist its pull, and opened to the first page. On the inside cover was an inscription in tidy handwriting.

'Being without a Bible is like going without SCRAN in battle.'

Linc chuckled. SCRAN: Stuff Cooked by the Royal Australian Navy. He shook his head and read on.

'This book will be food for your spirit that will help you stay strong. God's word will never let you down. You can build your life on it and know that when storms come, what you've built will remain standing.
As you begin your journey with God, know that

"No," Linc answered carefully, "dating implies a casual relationship. I want to court you with the intention of finding out where God may take this. I'm not fooling around with your heart."

Amelia's smile was shy, and it hardly touched the surface of how she felt about his request. "Yes Linc, I'd like that very much."

He released a relieved breath and grinned, revealing a straight row of pearly white teeth.

"And you won't need to transfer. I've been thinking for quite a while that I don't want to renew my contract. I just didn't expect circumstances like this to hurry the decision along." She dropped her gaze, her mind going back to that awful moment when Gareth Utano came at her with his weapon raised.

She squeezed her eyes shut tightly to block the pictures that flooded her awareness. The gentle pressure of Linc's hand over hers brought her back to the present.

"Sorry," she whispered and blinked back tears.

"Don't be. I expect the flash backs will be around for a while."

Amelia studied him. "Have you been getting them too?"

He rubbed his face and suddenly looked weary beyond his years. "More than I can count. But it's the nightmares that I hate the most. The ones where you die and..." He drew a suddenly shaky breath and shook himself free of the images that had clearly haunted his dreams. "You're here, and that's what matters the most. I don't want to waste this second chance God gave you. The second chance He gave me."

"Me either."

Linc reached out and tucked a wild strand of hair behind her ear. He then ran his fingers gently down her cheek. Amelia leaned into his touch with a sigh and soaked in the comfort he offered. A warm smile parted his lips and he tweaked her nose.

"Have I mentioned that I love the freckles on this adorable nose?"

Amelia's face heated and she smiled shyly in return.

He grinned and changed the topic. "Before we go any further, there's something I need to tell you."

Amelia watched the lightness in his eyes depart as swiftly as it had come. Gravity settled over him and she felt her muscles tense. What was wrong?

Linc focused on the floor at his feet. "I was involved with someone for quite a while. She panicked and left me just over five months ago after I proposed. It was only recently that I found out she was carrying my child. She died in childbirth."

Amelia was disappointed and also surprised by a touch of jealously that he had been with another woman. He had lived as the world lived, but empathy overrode her personal feelings. His sorrow was obvious. "And the child?"

"A baby girl. Yasmin." He chanced a look at her face and found only compassion. "It was before I met Jesus. I haven't lived the way He wanted me to, and I regret that. But unfortunately it's something I can't change. I *can* change my future. You'd be taking on a readymade family, and I'd want no less than total love and acceptance for Yasmin. I'll understand if you change your mind. It's a big ask."

Amelia considered his words carefully. He was right. It *was* a big ask. It was also something she had no doubt God could help with.

"Can I meet her?"

Relief flooded Linc's countenance and a slow smile relaxed his features. "I'll bring her in tomorrow if you'd like."

"Good. I love babies." She smiled and rested her head against the pillows behind her, exhaustion tugging at her body. She fought it.

"It's okay. You can sleep if you want to." Linc seemed to read her.

"But if I do, you'll leave." She smiled bashfully. "And I love having you here."

Linc reciprocated and held her hand upon the covers. "I'll stay awhile and watch you snore. How does that sound?"

"I don't snore. But the staying part sounds good." Her words were becoming slurred and her eyelids were heavy and drifting shut.

"Sleep well, Teddy." He gave her hand a gentle squeeze.

She fell asleep with a soft smile on her face.

28

Twelve Days Later:

Nethania used Padi's knife to mark off another day. Her slender fingers slid over the notches in the tree trunk. Her brows knit. There were eight groupings of five.

She sat back and stretched a leg before her and drew the other up to her chest. She looped her arms around it and linked her fingers. Her serene gaze swept across white sand to her left and her right, and then out to sea. A gentle smile touched her lips.

Where had the days gone? The passage of time had ceased to exist.

"It's odd Papa." She sensed her heavenly Father's presence closer than ever before. "I'm not anxious like I was to be rescued. In fact, I'm a little sad our forty days is up. I have so much more I want to learn from You. So much more I've yet to discover."

A soft breeze toyed with thick dark hair. The setting sun bounced off the ocean, engulfing everything in its golden glow. The sand began to take on an orange hue, and waxy leaves glinted in dusk's light. The sun's waning flame picked up natural red highlights in Nethania's hair and she smiled in pure delight. The sky was God's canvas and the light His brush. Now she too was part of His artwork.

Her eyes lit with wonder and filled with adoration. "Oh Papa, how I love you! Please, let us not leave? Let us stay?"

Ah daughter, His familiar voice resounded within the walls of her heart, *this is just the beginning of our journey. The best is yet to come. Trust Me.*

She smiled. Trust. It was something she had fought hard against tooth and nail those first two weeks. Yet as His marvellous provision continued pouring in every day, complete reliance had grown from small seeds to mountain moving proportions. "Yes Papa."

Rest child. I will watch over you.

Nethania's expression was one of pure contentment as she lay down and shuffled to get comfortable on a bed of leaves. She pulled large palm fronds over her and easily sank into a deep, restful sleep.

~

The doorbell rang. Amelia paused in front of the sofa, torn between answering it and her desperate need to sit down. Carrie breezed through the front hall toward the entrance.

"I'll get it Teddy. Go ahead and put your feet up."

Amelia smiled at her friend's use of her nickname. It hadn't taken long for it to rub off. She gingerly eased onto the burgundy suede couch, and one at a time, put

JAY .H. DEE

her feet up on the matching ottoman.

She had been released from hospital only three days ago. Although her health was improving, it did not take much to wear her out. This morning she had showered, dressed and eaten. She had even gone so far as to collect the Lonigan's mail from their box by the front gate. Now she felt as though she had run a marathon.

"How's our patient?"

Amelia heard Carrie's cheerful reply to the familiar masculine voice.

"Keeping me on my toes today. You *would* bring this adorable angel when I have to go out and can't have a cuddle!"

Amelia smiled and forced weary lids open. "Has Yasmin come to see me?"

"Yes, and she's brought a good looking sailor."

Amelia resisted a chuckle. Those were still painful.

Carrie poked her head around the lounge doorway. "I won't be long. I haven't got much to get down the street. Any last minute requests?"

Amelia twisted her head on the sofa to see her friend. "Chocolate biscuits?"

Carrie grinned. "I'll see what I can do." She disappeared into the hallway again and the front door opened and closed.

Linc wandered into the lounge carrying a tiny pink bundle. His large frame and muscular arms dwarfed the infant and Amelia smiled. He caught her gaze and grinned.

"It's good to see you up and about." He sat on the

189

couch so that he faced her.

Amelia held out her arms expectantly and he passed her the baby. She settled the infant against her good side and propped her arm with cushions. Yasmin yawned and stretched a small arm above her head. Her eyes remained closed and her arm lowered again as she drifted further into sleep. Such trust. Tears blurred Amelia's vision.

"What's wrong?"

Her gaze lingered on the tiny miracle snuggled against her. Linc had come to see her almost every day in hospital and for most of them, he had brought Yasmin. She had come to love the child.

"Teddy?"

Amelia mentally shook herself free of painful memories. The contrast was so blatant. She saw Gareth Utano pull the trigger, and herself aiming and firing. She could still see him bleeding on the floor of the RHIB in vivid detail.

Then there was Yasmin. The baby was trusting and wholly dependent. She responded to the love showered upon her with smiles and gurgles.

Amelia blinked back tears. "I want to give life, not take it away."

She chanced a look at his face and saw compassion. There was something else there too. She dropped her gaze, unsure of herself and what to make of his expression. His fingers tucked strands of lose hair behind her ear and gently brushed down her cheek in a gesture that had become familiar. She glanced up questioningly.

"Maybe I can help with that."

Amelia studied him carefully. "What are you suggest-ing?"

"Marry me?" he entreated softly.

She looked long into his unguarded eyes and found both tenderness and vulnerability. "Why?"

"Because I love you."

Four simple words, and yet they changed everything. Amelia released the breath she had unconsciously been holding in a shuddering sigh. More tears clouded her vision, only this time they were tears of joy.

"Yes."

Linc lifted her chin with a finger. A smile tugged at his lips as he held her hazel eyes captive. "Why?"

"Because I love you too."

He released her chin with a gentle stroke of his fin-ger. "That's a pretty good reason."

"Oh that's so romantic!"

The couple turned to find Carrie in the doorway. Her hand had gone to her heart and she wore a touched expression. Her eyes suddenly widened.

"I didn't mean to eavesdrop. I left my handbag." She pointed to the side table against the far wall. "I'm go-ing now." She snatched her bag and beat a hasty re-treat.

Linc and Amelia exchanged glances and burst out laughing. Amelia winced, gently held her sore stomach and squelched any further impulse.

"Take it easy there, Teddy. Do you want me getting

into trouble when Carrie gets back?"

"She's the one that made me laugh, not you."

"Yeah, but she'll blame me. I'm the one on duty watch."

Amelia smiled warmly into his sparkling green eyes. "I think you're doing a good job of taking care of me."

He grinned and winked. "Be sure to pass that onto the boss then, okay?"

"I will."

29

"Tell me, why do you want to go poking around in a sunken battleship?" Ollie's left hand held the wheel loosely while his right rested on the arm of his chair. He glanced at the young Japanese tourist on the bench against the wall.

"My grandfadder was sailor on dis ship."

Ollie was instantly intrigued. "Did he survive the war?"

Ra-kin Aiji shook his head.

"You and your dad are travelling to his resting place?"

"Yes."

Ollie could appreciate that. He had great respect for those who laid down their lives for their country in the service. An unreadable veil came over Ra-kin's face. The silence in the wheelhouse stretched and Ollie made another attempt at conversation.

"That was bad luck about the boat you hired."

Ra-kin's gaze remained fixed upon the ocean.

"You know, engine trouble and all."

No response. Ollie sighed. Tough crowd. He decided to take the hint.

They sailed for another half hour. The only dialogue was when Ra-kin's father wandered in from the deck.

He had a brief conversation with his son in fast, clipped Japanese before they both returned astern.

Ollie was glad to see them go. Most tourists who hired his charter were happy to be on holiday and generally talked nonstop. These two seemed on edge. For the life of him, Ollie couldn't work out why.

His musings were interrupted by an unhealthy sputter from the engine. It coughed, burped and lurched.

"What on earth?" He cut the power. What was that smell?

Dayne poked his concerned head out of the galley. "There's smoke coming from below."

Ollie scooted from his seat and followed Dayne to the engine room. "What could possibly be wrong? She's had a complete overhaul." He grabbed a fire extinguisher along the way just in case.

~

Nethania strode to the beach and packed her meagre gear. She had washed at the spring, determined not to smell like a stinky fisherman if she was to be rescued.

It was day forty-one. The odds of someone stumbling across her after forty days of isolation were unlikely. Her spirit, all the same, soared with faith. She had an inexplicable knowing that today was the day. She settled on the beach to watch and wait.

~

"Where do we go once we've split the dough? Won't people wonder where we got it from?" Trevor glanced at his comrades questioningly.

Bruno switched off the engine. "We'll figure that out soon enough. Let's just dig it up."

The boat bobbed gently in the calm island waters.

Garvey dropped the anchor. "Trev, lower the tinny."

~

"Ollie, look at this." Dayne waved him over.

Ollie moved away from the gauges. The oil gauge was low. Thankfully the engine wasn't overheated. The smoke seemed to be coming from oil that had spilled on the hot motor.

He was puzzled. They had left port with a full quota. He knelt beside Dayne and squinted through the smoky haze. Finally he saw what Dayne was pointing at. The nut that acted as a plug for the engine oil was missing.

"That was tight yesterday."

"It couldn't have worked loose," Dayne reasoned. "I was the one who changed the oil. Someone's deliberately drained it off."

The two men stared at one another grimly. Ollie's gaze lifted suspiciously to the hatch that led to the galley above. Who were their passengers? And why didn't someone want them poking around an old World War Two wreck?

~

Nethania strode through the forest along a path her own feet had worn. She had left her vigil for only twenty minutes to quench her thirst at the spring. However, as she drew near the beach, she could hear male voices on the breeze.

She halted ten paces from her campsite which was on the edge of the trees. Her stunned gaze alighted upon a figure crouched beside an evergreen. He was fingering the notches she had carved to mark the passage of time.

Several metres beyond him were two Asian men. One assessed the warmth of the coals in her fire pit. The older of the two held Padi's tin and was flipping slowly through the documents inside. The contents of the pack were now strewn at his feet on the dried leaves.

Nethania felt a spark of irritation. "Any particular reason why you feel free to rifle through my things? Especially since the site has clearly not been deserted."

The young Australian by the tree stood and spun. Surprised grey eyes met hers. Nethania's cool gaze shifted to the older gentleman. He had started in fright and turned. His expression hardened and she did not like the flicker of anger she saw.

He indicated the papers in his hand. "Where you get dese?"

One fine brow rose at his accusatory tone. "None of your business. Please give me the tin?" She held out her hand expectantly.

A standoff resulted.

The Aussie by the tree placed his hands on his hips and eyed his companion with mild irritation. "Give it back to her Mr. Aiji. I warned you not to touch any-thing."

The gentleman grudgingly replaced the lid. Nethania stepped forward and received the tin.

All of her ire was gone. "Are you any relation to Ma-hito Aiji?"

The younger Asian man walked to the side of the older, presumably his father. "He was my grandfadder."

She carefully studied the men. The older Mr. Aiji was inscrutable and he unnerved her. Her mind raced. Mr. Aiji and Mr. Kado were both after their father's sunken treasure.

The Australian stepped forward and offered his hand, effectively diffusing the situation. "Name's Ollie."

She shook it. "Nethania. I've been expecting you."

He gave her a quizzical look.

She shook her mind free of questions. "Excuse me. It's been a while since I've seen another person and I seem to have forgotten my manners."

Ollie's gaze swung to the marks on the tree and then back to her. "Nethania..." He puzzled momentarily, and appeared to be putting two and two together. "The life jacket from The Queen Maree... That was yours?"

Nethania smiled. "You found that hey?"

"Everyone thinks you're dead."

A mischievous sparkle lit her eyes. "Not hardly."

~

"So what's the word on Finn Cruikshank?" Linc had just entered the bridge and now leant against a support post.

Joshua rose from his chair. The ship was underway and headed for the open ocean. This was the second time in two months Linc did not want to leave. His reason was vastly different from his last voyage. This time he had left behind a cute brunette who had agreed to marry him.

Joshua clasped Linc's forearm in a hearty grip. "It's good to have you back Lieutenant."

He gave his commanding officer an easy going grin. "Good to be back. Although I admit I miss home already."

Joshua's eyes glimmered with secret knowledge. "Understandable."

Linc eyed his CO suspiciously. His relationship with Amelia was being kept under wraps until her resignation was official. She had only just filed the paperwork.

"Has Carrie Lonigan being talking with Joey by any chance sir?"

Joshua grinned and turned to look out the windshield. The bow sliced through the ocean with ease. "Nope. Jackie has."

Linc crossed his arms and smiled in amusement. "Figures. So what happened to Cruickshank?"

Jaffa swivelled in his chair at the communications desk. "The refugee woman we escorted to Cairns identified Utano from some photos."

Shep glanced over his shoulder from the navigation station. "The feds have gathered more evidence and made connections between the two. They've thrown the book at Finn."

"And the woman and her son? What happened to them?"

Joshua passed him a grim look. "They've been taken to a detention centre."

Sadness brought a heavy silence to the bridge. No one appeared thrilled by the state of affairs. The Christmas Island detention centre alone was filled to the point the government had put up some refugees in a local motel.

"So where are we headed on this rotation?"

This was clearly news to the crew, for each head in the room turned to the captain to hear the answer.

"A P3 Orion picked up several vessels to the north. We've been tasked to check out one headed for Ashmore Reef."

"Ashmore Reef?" Linc knew what that meant. "The gap between there and Indonesia isn't far."

"Which is why people smugglers use that route,"

Joshua concluded.

30

Nethania took a sip of her first coffee in over a month. She sighed with pleasure and closed her eyes to savour the robust mouthful. She remembered she had company and realised they must think her mad. She opened them again and swung a quick glance at her hosts. Sure enough, both Ollie and Dayne were watching her with amused expressions.

She smiled sheepishly. "You can't imagine how good this is."

Dayne grinned and leaned against the opposite wall. Ollie rested his arms on the table in the galley with a can of coke in his hands. Nethania sat across from him.

The Aiji men could be heard bickering on the deck in furious Japanese. Nethania had relented and allowed the men access to the tin. She could see no point in standing in their way when it related to their family. She had been on board now for about fifteen minutes.

Ollie's grey eyes were alight with a curious gleam. "What did you mean when you said you'd been expecting us?"

Nethania studied the mug in her hands and smiled. They would probably think her crazy, but she thought it worth at least attempting to explain. "When I first got to the island I was anxious and afraid."

She glanced up at the men. Both seemed attentive.

"All I could think about was Padi and Macca out there somewhere. I didn't know if they were dead or alive. Then I kept thinking about my family and what they would be going through when I didn't return. Finally I made my peace with God.

"You see, I walked away from Him seven months ago. Anyway, I was impatient to get off the island so I could set things right at home. Then God asked me for forty days."

Nethania studied her companions carefully. They both looked open and she wondered what they believed. "I'll admit I wasn't thrilled about it. But it's God and who can really argue?" She smiled wryly.

A half smile tugged at the corner of Ollie's mouth.

Dayne smiled in amusement. "My mum always says, He doesn't make us go against our will, He just makes us willing to go."

Nethania grinned. "Exactly. So there you have it. You arrived on day forty-one." A thoughtful look claimed her features. "I must confess that by the time forty days was up, part of me wanted it to last forever. I grew to love the solitude and the chance it gave me to commune with God."

Dayne's brows waggled. "Want us to put you back?"

Nethania laughed and took another sip of coffee. "Thanks for the offer, but no. I did miss modern comforts like showers, a flushing toilet and coffee." She held up her mug.

Ollie had an easy going chuckle that made her smile. "I'd love to sit and chat, but I'd better see if I can get onto any ships in the area." He slid off the bench and wandered toward the wheelhouse.

"Engine trouble," Dayne added in answer to Nethania's curious expression.

She smiled broadly. "So I'm just as stranded as I was before you showed up?"

Ollie paused in the doorway and passed her an amused look. "Yeah, but you've got running water, coffee and a flushing toilet."

~

Trevor looked at Bruno questioningly. The skipper dumped another load of gold on the wheelhouse floor and ignored the radio call for help.

Trevor was in a quandary. "Shouldn't we respond?"

Bruno levelled him with look that said he was nuts. "You answer that radio an' you'll give away our position. Folks'll start askin' questions 'bout what we've got on board. Do yourself a favour an' learn to keep shut."

Trevor's eyes spat fire over the demeaning reprimand. He bit back the hot retort on his tongue. He'd be a fool to cross his boss, especially now that he knew what he was capable of.

~

"Dayne, there's a fishing boat over on Murphy." Ollie passed a pair of binoculars to his first mate.

They were at the railing on the deck. Dayne received the binoculars and lifted them to his eyes. He aimed them in the direction Ollie was pointing. He knew the sight Dayne was seeing right now.

Moored just off a rocky outcrop on the distant island was a white fishing boat. There seemed to be no life on board, although there was a small tinny floating at the base of the rocks.

"Whoever it is, they've gone ashore. That'll be why they haven't responded." Dayne lowered the binoculars and handed them back to Ollie.

"How far do you suppose it is?"

Dayne exhaled slowly. "A couple of kilometres. You're not thinking of sailing us there?"

Ollie's gaze narrowed in thought. "No. We were pushing it to get here. I was considering taking the dingy." He glanced at Dayne.

"I know there's no stopping you mate. I'll inflate it." He headed inside straight for the galley.

Ollie followed him. He stopped his friend in the process of lifting the lid off the bench seat to retrieve the inflatable life raft. "Dayne." Ollie lowered his voice. "I don't trust our guests. I need you to stay and keep an eye on them."

The other man studied him in silence for several minutes and lowered the lid, leaving the dingy inside. "Okay. Although you know as well as I do that it's not wise to go alone."

Movement in the doorway between the wheelhouse and the galley drew their attention. Nethania stood with arms crossed and an unfazed expression observing them.

"I'll go."

Ollie exchanged glances with Dayne. Dayne tilted his head in question and one shoulder lifted in a shrug.

Ollie met her even stare. "We'll have to row."

Nethania's eyes sparkled mischievously. "Don't worry, when you get tired you can pass your oar to me."

Dayne laughed and went back to digging through the compartment beneath the bench. Ollie grinned and headed out on deck to inform his passengers.

~

"What kind of engine trouble are we talking about?" Nethania maintained a steady rhythm on her oar.

Ollie kept pace beside her. "Someone drained most of the oil from our motor this morning, and stole the spare canister we were carrying."

Nethania noted the irritated edge to his voice. "Why would someone do that?"

Ollie's determined gaze lingered on The Dream Catcher behind them. It was slowly becoming nothing more than a blip in the distance. "That's what I'd like to know."

Nethania's muscles were starting to tire. She forged on regardless. She could see the fishing boat Ollie had mentioned moored by a rocky outcrop not far away.

31

Amelia opened the front door to Carrie and Lon's home and blinked. She stared in stunned surprise at the six foot male on her doorstep. Anxious lines furrowed his brow, and freckles dotted his fair skin. His features were not altogether striking, but they were more familiar to her than her own.

Her mouth eased into a smile. "Paul."

He frowned and stuck his fists on his hips. "What's this about getting shot at? We only let you join the navy 'cos we figured you couldn't get into much trouble working on an engine."

"*You* let me join the navy? Paul Jones, you're still as bossy as the day is long."

Her older brother grinned and stepped over the threshold. At the same time he gathered her into an embrace. Amelia's heart warmed. It was the first gentle hug she could ever recall receiving from him. Finally he stepped back and held her at arm's length.

"You scared the living daylights out o' me. Don't do it again or I'll break your neck."

Amelia levelled him with a dry look. "Don't worry, there will be no repeats. Where's Jen and the boys?" She peered around his solid frame to the roadside and could see only his empty blue Holden Rodeo.

"They couldn't come. James has school and Luke has

kinder." Paul's usually sparkling eyes studied her intently. "We figured air travel might be a bit risky, so I drove up. I'm here to take you home."

For the first time Amelia could remember, she felt torn. She desperately wanted to be with her family, but to go home would put her two states away from Linc and Yasmin.

She was suddenly aware that they were standing on the doorstep. "Come in, Paul."

He closed the door behind him and followed her to the living room. Carrie was at work and Lon was still at sea. Amelia had spoken of her family often, although she hadn't expected any of them to show up on Carrie's doorstep. She was thrilled Paul had.

He dropped into an arm chair, his gaze doing an appreciative sweep of the room. "Your friends have a nice place."

Amelia smiled. "It *is* lovely." She eased carefully onto the couch and adjusted the pillows behind her.

Paul missed nothing. "You healing up well?"

"The doctor is happy. My stitches will come out in a couple of days. I'll probably be sore for a while though."

They regarded one another quietly for several minutes. Paul was the one to break the silence.

"Okay, who is he and how the heck did it happen so fast?"

Amelia stifled a laugh. Her brother's were both protective to a fault. "Let me guess, Steven put you up to this?"

A half smile tugged at Paul's mouth. "He did say I should look the guy over and give him 'the talk'. From your conflabs with Mum, she's basically floating around the house with giddiness. Dad wants to meet him. Steve just wants to give him a right hook."

Amelia frowned. Her oldest brother never failed to have her baffled. "Why?"

"Oh just a warning to treat you right I'd say." It was said with such a matter-of-fact tone.

Amelia sighed. There was no way she was bringing Linc home if that was the case. He'd drop her like a hot scone the moment he encountered her brothers. She was grateful he was still at sea. "And you?"

Paul shrugged. "You look happy. I mean, I can see you're not one hundred percent, but you've got this look about you..."

A lively glint did indeed light her hazel eyes on a regular basis when she thought of her intended. She knew it was there even now.

"What can I tell you, Paul? I've never met anyone who made me want to settle down. Linc is special." She shrugged.

There was so much more she could say, but wouldn't. Her brother had a serious side, but more often than not, anything she shared was later ammunition for family jesting.

"It's not just 'cos you think he's the only guy that'll ever ask?"

The question was spoken gently, and Paul's eyes were kind. All the same, it hurt to be reminded of the past. There had been a time she believed no one would ever notice her. Then she had moved past that hurdle and delved into a career she loved and hobbies that took up her time and gave her a sense of fulfilment.

Church, friends and family filled the gaps in her life to a point she had ceased to long for a mate. Then Linc had happened along and her contentment with the status quo had gone out the window.

"I was happily single, Paul. It's not like I needed a man to complete me. The fact the right one has come along is a blessing. I always told you guys that when the right man showed up I'd just know."

Paul assessed her in silence and finally relaxed. Amelia supposed he read her calm certainty and the peace that surrounded her like an aura. She also thought he might have picked up on the hint of steel beneath her gentle manner. She knew her mind, and in her own quiet way, made sure her family were aware of it on a regular basis. If she didn't, she was sure her brothers would try to run her life.

"Fair enough. Just as long as he deserves you, I'm cool with it."

Amelia rolled her eyes. "If you and Steve are the judges, no one would ever make the cut."

Paul held up his hands in his defence. "It's not my fault I have an exceptional sister. I've got a job to do as a big brother."

Amelia smiled warmly and blinked back moisture. That was the closest she'd heard him come to saying 'I love you.' The men in her life were far too macho for sentimentality. Although after her dad's heart attack the year before, he had softened and begun to show affection more.

Amelia supposed almost losing her had impacted her family more than she realised. It had certainly changed her. "That's the nicest thing you've said to me in ages."

He looked uncomfortable and shifted in his seat. "Yeah well, don't get too used to it. I can't have you going all schmaltzy on me. I think this counts as my once a year sappy moment."

Amelia chuckled. "I missed you."

Paul grinned at her. "You too, grease monkey."

~

Nethania stood on the deck of the fishing vessel and stared in awe. Around her and Ollie were a couple of small eskies and two crates of gold and jewels. Although it was obvious from their condition that they had been submerged for a very long time, they were still breathtaking to behold.

"I've got a really bad feeling about this."

Nethania glanced sideways at Ollie. "Me too." All of the documents from Padi's tin flashed before her mind's eye in a millisecond and a sinking feeling tugged at her stomach.

Was this what Padi had been after? And Ra-kin Aiji back there... Was this his grandfather's treasure?

"Ollie, I think this is what Sadamu and Ra-kin Aiji and

Dake Kado are after."

Ollie frowned at her. "Who's Dake Kado?"

"He's the guy who funded Padi's and my research. I figured out too late that he was funding it because during World War Two his father had discovered sunken treasure from a Dutch ship, The Hildegard. I think Padi was looking for it on his behalf."

"You're not making much sense."

"I'll explain later. Let's just say that I believe we've found the reason why you've got engine trouble." Nethania hastened to the rear of the boat and climbed over and into the dingy.

"Who are these guys?"

Nethania heard Ollie's soft murmur as a sense of urgency came over her. "I don't think we want to stay and find out. There's a reason they weren't answering their radio, and it's sitting there in all its glory." She pointed to the loot. "There's not much some people won't do to protect something like that."

Ollie gave the spoils one last glance and climbed in beside her. "I'd still like to know who owns this boat and where they got all that gold."

Nethania pushed off and took up her oar. "I'll fill you in on my theory while we row."

32

Linc sank into the chair at the computer desk in the office with a sigh. It had been a hectic day. He powered the computer and replayed events, the biggest of which was intercepting a refugee boat on the verge of sinking along the north coast.

The people on board were starving and dehydrated. The boat had been out of fuel and would never have made the mainland. They were currently being tended to by the crew and would be delivered to the Oceanic Viking, a ship that would ferry the asylum seekers to Christmas Island for processing.

Linc checked his email. He admired his update from Jaclyn. The picture of Yasmin in a pink lacy dress and a cute headband with a flower on it, was adorable. He moved to the next email and was thrilled to see Amelia's address. He clicked and began to read.

'Linc, I'm not sure what to do. My brother is here and wants to take me home. I want to go, but then I'll be so far away from you and Yasmin. At the same time, I don't want to trespass upon Carrie and Lon's hospitality any longer. I don't have a place of my own and I'm not sure exactly what our plans are. We haven't really set a date. I'm well enough to handle the drive to Victoria. I don't want to jeopardise us with distance. What do you think?'

He frowned. The missive was underpinned by a great amount of uncertainty. She was rattled and feeling insecure. He smiled and began a reply.

'Teddy, relax. You need to be with your family. That's totally understandable. Yasmin and I will hop the first flight to Melbourne when I get back to port. I'd like to meet your family. We'll set a date then and make our plans more concrete.

I'm not messing around with your heart. I *will* marry you. The when and where we'll discuss in a couple of weeks. Until then, rest in the knowledge this sailor loves you and will chase you down to the ends of the earth... or to Melbourne. Whichever is furthest.

Love Linc.'

He hit send and prayed for her right then and there. The realisation his prayer went from his lips to God's ears, and from God's hands into Amelia's life, was a great comfort. Although he couldn't be there to hold her, his Heavenly Father could. He smiled and shutdown the computer. He needed some serious sleep if he was to go on watch at dawn.

"They know."

Garvey studied Bruno's intent gaze following the progress of the couple rowing away from their vessel. "How do you figure that?"

Trevor released his end of the last crate of gold. Garvey, who was holding the other side, lowered it to the ground as well. It let out a thud and a jingle of coins. Bruno had gone before them and they had just caught up with him at the edge of the tree line.

"I heard the woman refer to Padi and Dake Kado and the sunken treasure they were after. Trust me, they know."

Bruno's hard eyes landed upon them. In it was reflected a coldness that sent a shudder down Garvey's spine.

"They don't know we killed Padi. No one does."

Bruno's dangerous gaze swung to Trevor. "If one word gets out 'bout this loot, everyone'll figure it out like that." He snapped his fingers. "Only a fool leaves a trail for others to follow."

Garvey swallowed hard. There wasn't much he wouldn't do to protect their newfound wealth. On the other hand, he didn't savour killing again.

A look of dread passed over Trevor's features. "Are you sayin' we gotta kill 'em?"

Garvey indicated the gold at their feet with an extended arm and a sarcastic expression. "You wanna share this?"

Trevor glared at him. "Fine. Kill 'em then. Kill 'em all!" He lifted his end of the crate, all the while muttering. "But once I get my share, I'm findin' some quiet place down the coast, an' ain't nobody's gunna make me do anythin' like that again."

Bruno and Garvey exchanged grins. Garvey took up his end of the burden and Bruno led the way to the boat.

~

"So you believe this is the sunken treasure from the Hildegard, which was discovered by the ancestors of Sadamu Aiji and Dake Kado?"

Nethania panted as she rowed hard beside Ollie. "Why else would you find centuries old gold and jewels in this area? It's the only explanation. When we get back to the boat, you'll have to read the documents in Padi's tin."

She heard an engine rumble to life in the distance and noted the vessel they had left behind teaming with life. It was roughly two hundred metres away, and three men were moving around. One was casting off, another dragging crates below deck, and a third was at the helm.

Ollie's line of sight followed hers. "How do you want to play this? Wave and pretend we don't know what they're carrying?"

A sardonic smile tugged at Nethania's lips. "Just row faster will you?"

Water surged around the dingy as greater effort from both propelled it forward.

"Uh-oh."

At Ollie's mutter, Nethania turned from looking over her shoulder at The Dream Catcher, to the fishing vessel they had left minutes ago.

"They're coming straight for us." Ollie intensified his labours and his biceps rippled and strained to full capacity.

"Papa, we could use some help?"

Ollie slid her a curious look. "Huh?"

"I was just praying for a little assistance," Nethania confessed. She was unused to this kind of physical exertion and was running out of breath. Swimming and jogging around the island was one thing. Rowing hard several kilometres was another.

"Good. I'm doing the same."

Nethania looked at Ollie in surprise. "You're a praying man?"

The expression he flashed her suggested he found her timing for a personal discussion absurd. "Absolutely."

Nethania was delighted, and her sparkling blue eyes showed it. "I'm glad to hear it." Her eyes narrowed. "Who do you pray to?"

Ollie's eyes held a hint of humour. "God the Father, God the Son, and God the Holy Spirit. Does that give you any clues as to what religion I am?"

Nethania grinned. "A follower of The Way?"

"If by that you mean a follower of Jesus Christ, then yes."

She laughed and Ollie looked at her strangely.

"Aren't you a little scared that boat is gaining on us?"

Nethania shrugged as she rowed. "I'm not happy about it. But there's no reason I should fear a man, or three for that matter. What can they do to me?"

Ollie raised one brow. "Kill you."

Nethania brushed his remark aside. "And then what? They can't touch me in heaven."

Ollie just shook his head. "Well I'd just as soon hang around this earth a bit longer if that's alright with you. Can't you row any faster?"

"My arms feel like they're going to fall off. I'm going as fast as I can."

The fishing vessel was bearing down upon them. And gaining speed.

"I think they plan to run us over."

"You think?"

At Ollie's sarcastic tone, it was Nethania's turn to raise a brow. "You *are* touchy."

"Some maniac is about to run us down! Touchy is the tip of the iceberg!"

Nethania watched as the boat sped the last ten metres. The skipper's face was visible through the windshield. A callous smile accompanied a pair of malicious eyes as waves broke at the bow. Three metres, two...

"I don't know about you, but I'm not going down with this ship." Nethania tossed her oar aside.

Ollie's eyes widened and he did the same. "Jump!"

Simultaneously, they dove into the water, one either direction of the bow about to collide with them. Moments later the vessel collected their dingy. It popped and was tossed aside in the wash from the boat.

Nethania surfaced and watched the vessel slow. It passed and her gaze locked with a miscreant grinning at her from the stern. Looking scruffy and unkempt, he tossed her a life buoy.

"Sorry 'bout that."

She scowled at him and then searched the waves around her for Ollie. He was nowhere to be seen. Had he been hit or encountered the propeller? All she could see was the mangled dingy partially floating nearby.

"Grab on. Don't wanna drown do ya?"

Nethania snatched the life buoy, scowl still in place. "That wouldn't be an issue if you hadn't hit us! What's your problem?"

The boat had come to a stop and was idling roughly. He wound her in, hand over hand. The menace dragged her out of the water. The deck was no longer cluttered with crates or eskies of treasure.

"The boss reckons *you* might be our problem. Where's your boyfriend?"

Nethania stood with hands on her knees, catching her breath and dripping seawater all over the deck. "He's not my boyfriend. And you had better find him!"

A clatter and a loud splash drew their attention. The man in front of her turned to investigate. His eyes widened as a wet form came at him swift and silent. He was caught in the face by a fist and stumbled back against the stern rail.

Nethania watched in wide-eyed astonishment as Ollie spun for the wheelhouse at the same time the skipper exited. The rough looking character swung a knife in a wild arch. Ollie caught the hand welding the weapon and disarmed him. The knife clattered to the deck.

Nethania snatched it up. Ollie flipped his assailant over his shoulder onto the deck and pinned him face to the floor.

Where had he learned to fight like that?

"Garvey, get the girl!" the skipper demanded in a surly growl.

Nethania caught movement from the corner of her eye. The sailor at the stern was wiping blood from a split lip. Menacing brown eyes studied the red liquid on his hand and turned angrily on her.

"I can turn the other cheek only so many times. I've only got two you know," she remarked and tightened her grip on the knife.

Its steel blade was at least six inches long and the rubber grip covering the handle was moulded to the shape of her hand. Could she really use it? Her moment of hesitation cost her.

Garvey lunged for the knife. While his left arm grabbed her around the shoulders, his right wrested the blade away and held it to her neck. His body pressed against her back and her nose crinkled at his odour.

"Don't you ever wash?"

He tightened his grip and she could feel the blade begin to slice tender skin. "If it's any help, I probably wouldn't have used that anyway," she choked out.

"Yeah, but I will." Pungent breath warmed her ear and set her stomach rolling. "After I've had some fun with ya first."

She was about to die, and rather unpleasantly by the sound of it. *Here I come, Papa!*

"Let her go!" Ollie released the skipper and stepped back, breathing hard and looking like a bear being robbed of its cubs.

There was some splashing from the stern and the lanky third sailor sloshed toward them rubbing a bruised jaw. Ollie kept his gaze riveted on Nethania.

While the skipper picked himself up off the deck, the sandy haired man who had been tossed overboard landed a nasty blow to Ollie from behind. He crumpled to the deck and remained motionless. Nethania cringed.

The knife blade eased somewhat and she breathed a sigh of relief. "That was unnecessary, don't you think?"

"Shut your trap!"

Bad breath wafted to her nostrils and she wrinkled her nose. "You seriously need to brush your teeth."

The knife tightened. "I said shut up!"

Nethania inhaled and held onto it. With one eye closed and the other squinting, she waited for the final incision. It didn't come.

He released her and shoved her toward the wheelhouse. She had to step over Ollie's unconscious body to reach the entrance.

"I'll take care o' this one."

Garvey's sinister tone sent a spiral of fury through her.

"Hurry it up Garv," the skipper growled. "We gotta get rid o' anyone else on that boat over yonder. Trevor, tie this bloke up. We'll dispose of 'im when we get there. No one'll ever find a few unmarked graves on an island in the middle o' nowhere."

Nethania heard his barked command as she was thrust into the wheelhouse and down a small set of stairs. They passed a galley and she was shoved into the sleeping quarters beyond. She stumbled and caught her balance on the bunk against the wall.

She turned and stared at the nasty piece of work closing the door. He faced her and a sadistic smile tugged at the corners of his mouth.

33

Dayne pulled the binoculars from his eyes and muttered angrily under his breath. He picked up the radio, keyed the mic and issued a mayday. No answer was forthcoming.

The fishing vessel, however, steered his direction and powered its engine. They had heard and were coming for him too. He dug in his pocket for his cell phone and held it high. No reception. He tried a text message and then an email. Both returned.

"Blast!"

He tucked his phone in his pocket and ransacked the galley for every item that could be considered a weapon. He thrust them into Padi's backpack by the table and shouldered it.

Dayne jogged onto the deck. "You two, come with me!"

The gentlemen talking at the stern turned to look at him with confused expressions. The oldest noted the urgency in Dayne's actions as he stepped over the rear railing.

"What is wrong?"

"Someone just ran down Ollie and Nethania. Ollie tried to fight them off but from what I could see, they've got them both. Now they're coming for us."

Dayne dropped into the shallow water at the back of

the boat and swam toward the shore.

The youngest stood at the rail looking both alarmed and perplexed. "Where are you going?"

The two men reluctantly climbed down from the boat into the water and swam after Dayne. The water was clear and the white sand beneath them visible. It wouldn't take much before they would be able to wade ashore.

Dayne tossed his reply over his shoulder. "You're both going to hide inland while I get Ollie and Nethania back."

~

Nethania's skin started to crawl as she stared into eyes taken over by evil.

Jesus, the price for my life to purchase me back from the evil one was blood. You took that cost and paid it with Your own. I plead the blood You shed as protection over me. I'm Yours. You protect Your own, right? I'm safe under the shadow of Your wings, am I not?

Garvey moved close, one menacing step at a time. He was enjoying being the cat and her the mouse. He reached forth his hand and panic rose within her and exploded in an indignant shout.

"You can't touch me! I'm covered in feathers!"

Garvey froze. His startled expression communicated clearly that she had gone crazy. She leant away from him and her hands came up to shield herself.

"I'm covered in His feathers and you can't touch me!"

He backed away and cursed. "She's ravin' mad!" he muttered to himself and opened the door.

He slammed it shut behind him and Nethania heard footsteps retreat. She sank absently onto the edge of the bed and hugged her midsection. It was then she realised she was shaking from head to foot. So much for fearing no man!

~

Dayne surfaced near the stationary fishing vessel while two of its crew stepped over onto The Dream Catcher. One man had sandy coloured hair and the other a murky unwashed brown. One was lanky and the other well muscled with a slight paunch. They went below deck to search, each armed with a knife.

Dayne carefully climbed aboard the fishing boat and slunk past the wheelhouse. At the stern was a strong looking man, roughly in his fifties, with his hands on the railing. He was watching The Dream Catcher. On the floor nearby with wrists and feet bound was Ollie. A gag was stretched taut across his mouth and tied at the nape. Dayne ignored him momentarily and crept straight for the villain at the rail.

Water dripped steadily from his shorts and t-shirt. The sound, although soft, was sufficient to alert the skipper to his presence. He was just turning when

Dayne grabbed him from behind around the neck with two arms. It was a hold from his past he had hoped he would never have to use again.

He counted specific seconds as the man struggled in vain. Circulation ceased and unconsciousness was swift in following. The man sagged under his grip and he dropped him onto the deck.

Dayne moved to Ollie's side and met his friend's urgent gaze. He removed the gag and then went to work on the ropes binding his wrists and his feet. The knife in his belt did the trick.

"Nethania." Ollie's words were slurred, suggesting concussion. "Where is she?"

"I'll get her. Tie that mongrel up." He indicated the unconscious man sprawled nearby.

Ollie got to his knees and grabbed a fist full of ropes. He blinked several times and tried to focus. Dayne suspected dizziness might be the cause. He helped him to his feet.

Dayne watched him stumble and regain his balance before dropping to a knee beside the downed man with ropes in hand. He glanced at The Dream Catcher and calculated they had only a minute more, maybe less.

He headed below in search of Nethania.

~

Nethania rose from the edge of the bunk and

watched the handle turn carefully. The door opened silently and Dayne stepped in. Her hands dropped to her sides and she sighed in relief.

"He said you were coming."

Dayne's brows furrowed. "Who?" He took her by the hand and led her topside.

Was Dayne a believer like Ollie? He might think her nuts if she tried to explain her conversation with her heavenly Father. "Never mind. How's Ollie."

"Alive. Are you okay?"

"Pure as the driven snow, thank God."

"Wanna tell me what this was all about?" He peered through the wheelhouse at The Dream Catcher. The deck was empty.

Nethania noted the skipper sprawled unconscious on the floor of the fishing vessel. Ollie was tying off the knot that bound his feet to his hands. Relief flooded her at the sight of her new friend.

Dayne pulled her toward the starboard rail, swung one leg over and then the other. He let go and slid over the edge into the water with minimal splash. Ollie joined her at the rail and silently indicated that she follow. She obeyed. In seconds all three were in the water and swimming for the shore.

The breakers were small and easy to navigate. Nethania's feet found the bottom and she trailed her two rescuers up the beach and into the jungle. All the while she wondered at the history of the two men with her. That they were more than simple fishermen was glaringly obvious.

HIDDEN

34

Garvey cursed and shook Bruno's shoulder. The skipper roused. Garvey slit the knot binding his hands and feet and helped pull him upright.

"What happened?"

Bruno rubbed his neck. He swallowed with a painful grimace. "Dunno. I was watchin' you blokes when someone grabbed me from behind."

Garvey pointed to where their captive had been. "Was it that blighter? Did he get loose?"

Bruno's brows drew together and he squinted at the bright sunlight in his face. "He couldn't 'ave. He's got help."

Trevor emerged from the wheelhouse. "I checked below. She's gone."

"Was it 'er?" Even as he asked the question, Garvey knew it was not possible. Aside from the fact she didn't have the muscle to render a big man like Bruno unconscious, she had been intimidated by him earlier and hesitant to use a knife, even if it meant saving her own life.

Bruno scowled at him. "It weren't no woman, I tell ya that! Whoever grabbed me knew what they were doin'. He had some kind 'o special trainin'."

Garvey stood and helped his boss onto unsteady legs. He was liking this situation less and less.

Trevor eyed them both with a large amount of uncertainty. "Let's just cut our losses an' get out o' 'ere
with the gold."

Bruno sent him a murderous look. "Ain't nobody's
gunna do that to me an' get away with it! Garv, there's
a couple o' rifles an' a handgun in the lock box beneath
my bunk. Get 'em."

Trevor's features drained of colour and his eyes widened. Garvey gritted his jaw and stomped down into
the belly of the boat. This time he agreed wholeheart-
edly with Bruno.

Even if they hadn't needed to destroy all witnesses
to the gold they were carrying, he would still want to
get his hands on the men who had done this. They had
messed with the boss and with him. It was now a matter of pride.

~

Once under the cover of the jungle, Dayne crouched
behind some undergrowth and studied the two boats
bobbing in the calm azure ocean a couple of hundred
metres away. Ollie dropped to the ground a few metres
further inland, his back to a stout tree and sat with legs
slightly bent at the knees. He rubbed the knot on the
back of his skull and grimaced.

Nethania did not miss the way he deliberately blinked, as though to rid himself of dizziness. She knelt
before him, and turned his head to have a look at his

injury. A lump was already forming behind his right ear. There was no blood, but that did not seem to matter. He clearly had concussion.

He took her left hand. "Are you okay?"

She sat back and met his anxious gaze in surprise. She read the question he did not want to ask and a flush crept up her neck into her cheeks. "He didn't touch me."

Tension visibly left his shoulders. He gave her hand a squeeze and released it. "What changed his mind?"

Nethania's blush deepened and she dropped her gaze to her feet. Dayne turned to listen, obviously curious.

"I told him he couldn't touch me because I'm covered in feathers. He thought I was crazy and left." She shrugged, but couldn't help feeling ridiculous admitting this to two very handsome men.

Dayne's frown deepened. Ollie's mouth hitched up in a grin, but his eyes held more questions.

Nethania grew defensive. "Well I am aren't I? Scripture says I'm safe beneath the shadow of God's wings."

Ollie glanced at Dayne and chuckled softly.

Dayne grinned and shook his head. "That's a very literal translation."

Nethania could not resist a smile. "I'm unharmed despite that man's intentions aren't I?"

"True." Dayne's gaze went back to the men moving about the boat deck.

"Where's Mr. Aiji and his son?" Ollie blinked a few times and squinted at his friend.

Nethania wondered if his vision was blurry. That wasn't a good sign.

"I sent them inland to hide." Dayne suddenly scowled. "Those men have guns."

"What?" Ollie struggled onto his feet, stumbled and crossed to where Dayne crouched.

The two eyed the fishing vessel. Nethania knelt behind them and peered over Ollie's shoulder. Dayne was right. The one called Garvey was carrying two rifles from the wheelhouse. He passed one to the skipper and they began checking chambers and loading magazines. The other man Ollie had pitched overboard was standing in the wheelhouse doorway. He was stuffing a handgun into his belt.

"What do we do now?" Nethania glanced between her two companions.

"Let's fetch my pack and find the Aiji's," Dayne suggested. "I've got a few knives."

"We need to come up with a plan on the way," Ollie offered and stood. He wavered and Nethania automatically shot out a hand to grab his arm and steady him.

He couldn't help but notice her worried expression and passed her a smile. "I've had worse than this. I'll be fine."

Nethania did not comment, but she did wonder.

"Come on, it's this way." Dayne indicated the direction they should take.

Ollie gestured for Nethania to precede him. She gave him one last uncertain glance and followed Dayne.

~

"What's our plan?" Garvey shouldered his .223 and moved to the stern where Trevor had the tinny launched.

Bruno snapped the bolt of his .303 shut. "We don't give 'em a chance for hand to hand combat. We pick 'em off at a distance."

Garvey grinned.

"Trev, go sabotage their radio. Sooner or later they'll try to get back to their boat. Use the Smith and Wesson if they do."

Trevor shifted uncomfortably from one foot to the other. "How long is this gunna take?"

"We'll be back by dark." Bruno passed Garvey and stepped down into the tinny.

His second in command followed. Trevor sighed. There was no use arguing when Bruno and Garvey had set their minds to something.

35

Nethania watched Dayne share out a number of knives and blunt objects between him and Ollie. The business-like manner with which they dispatched the task and discussed plans made her head spin. How could they be so matter-of-fact about their situation?

Sadamu and Ra-kin were arguing in Japanese as they sat nearby on a fallen tree. They gestured to Ollie and Dayne on occasion and she wondered what they were saying.

Her gaze returned to her new friends. "Where did you both serve?"

Ollie tucked his second blade in his waistband and glanced over at her. She had her back against a large tree and her arms crossed over her chest. Dayne's eyes darkened at the mention of military service.

"I'm ex-navy," Ollie offered.

Nethania met Dayne's intense gaze questioningly.

"Army," was all he would say.

Nethania sensed a story there but wisely backed off. "Now what?"

"The hunted become the hunters."

Dayne's simple comment caused a shudder to run down her spine. She couldn't reconcile between Jesus' command to love and their need to protect themselves by killing. The conflict must have shown in her eyes, because Ollie's face softened.

"Evil men prevail when good men do nothing, Nethania. If I can spare the lives of those men, I will. Either way, I won't allow them to take yours, or ours for that matter, just because the Bible says to love. If you love, you must also hate the evil deed. I'm not showing love if I don't do all in my power to stop evil."

His reasoning was new to her, and Nethania knew it would take some time for her to resolve the matter in her heart. Not sure what to think, she refrained from comment.

"What do you want me to do?"

Ollie held her gaze steadily. "Hide, and don't come out whatever you hear."

Her eyes widened and her heart felt sick. What if something happened to them? "Please be careful?"

Ollie closed the distance between them and gently took her by the upper arms. "We will. Just please stay hidden? We can't focus on what needs to be done if you're in danger. Okay?"

She nodded.

He held her gaze and gave her a reassuring smile. "Good."

Nethania was struck by his kindness. He genuinely cared. She hadn't felt cared about by another human being like that in a long time. Only by her parents. "I know some good places to hide. I'll take the Aiji's up the central mountain. There's a nice overhang that overlooks the beach for kilometres. Probably a World War Two relic. We'll be able to see if anyone approaches us without being seen ourselves."

Ollie dropped his hands and nodded. "That sounds like a great plan. Which direction is it?"

Nethania pointed north.

"We'll come find you when it's over," Dayne assured. "Ollie, let's go."

Nethania watched them fade into the jungle on silent feet. Ollie glanced back at her one last time and ushered her with a hand gesture to go. She moved away from the tree and strode toward the two arguing men.

"Come with me, and for crying out loud, hush up!"

Sadamu stood and eyed her cautiously. "We want my fadder's gold. Your friends, dey will get it?"

"No. They've got three armed men to deal with. I suggest you follow me and we lay low for a while."

"We do tings our own way. We not be told what to do anymore."

Nethania looked to the younger of the pair, who rose slowly from the fallen tree. "And you? Do you have a death wish too?"

"We did not come halfway around da world to see dose men steal from us. Your friends, dey want da gold too."

Nethania stared at him and marvelled that greed could so taint basic common sense. "No. They just want to get help and stop those men."

"We get to da odder boat wiff da gold. We call for help. You hide if you want to."

Nethania watched in stunned paralysis as the two

men spoke to each other in fast Japanese and strode back the way they had come. She stood in the forest alone in indecision.

"Papa, what do I do?"

Will you trust Me?

"Of course."

Accept the things you cannot change, and change the things you can.

Nethania pondered that thought. She couldn't choose for the Aiji's or for Ollie and Dayne. She could not change the course of action they had all chosen. She could, however, choose for herself.

"I can do more than hide, Papa."

I will be with you.

With a determined glint in her eyes, she slunk after the men on stealthy feet. She knew this island like the back of her hand. She could be of more use to Ollie and Dayne than they realised.

~

Dayne silently passed Ollie the binoculars. They were concealed in the undergrowth metres from the beach. Ollie surveyed the two boats not far from the shore. The fishing vessel appeared to be empty, as did their own. However, a head appeared nervously over the side of their charter at the stern every few minutes.

"He's waiting for us."

Ollie saw what Dayne meant and then studied the

beach. He pointed out drag marks on the sand to their right and kept his voice to a whisper. "Two have come ashore and hidden a tinny in the trees. I can see two sets of footprints."

"We can't go out in the open. That's what they're counting on." Dayne nodded toward the tracks. "Let's follow those two. I'd feel a whole lot better if I knew where they were."

"Me too. Why don't we-" Ollie froze. He could hear footsteps crunching dried twigs and leaves.

He and Dayne automatically melded into the trees and waited. Muffled voices drifted on the gentle breeze. Suddenly they stopped. Ollie moved carefully so that he could see down the beach. Fifty metres away, a flash of colour caught his eye along the tree line. Sadamu Aiji stepped out onto the beach.

Ollie's breath left him in a rush. What was the man thinking? He watched helplessly as the older man jogged down the sand and into the waves. A shot rang out loud and clear from their boat. He fell with a large splash into the water and did not move.

The second flash of colour dashed from the jungle in a panic, straight for his father. Before Ollie could even open his mouth to object, Dayne charged from the trees toward the young man. He watched in dread as another shot was fired.

A bullet caught the young man in the chest. It threw him backward and he landed in the sand. He struggled to his knees. Dayne finally reached him. He grabbed the wounded man around the waist and practically dragged him up the beach. A third sounded and a fourth.

Ollie was horrified when Dayne went down. He had to draw the gunfire away from his friend. How many bullets did the shooter have left? From what he could see with the binoculars, he was using an older pistol, not a rifle. That meant six shots. Two to go. Could he dodge two bullets and buy Dayne enough time to drag himself into the trees which were three metres away?

~

Nethania's hands clutched her head and her mouth was open. Her voice refused to work. She was frozen. Both the Aiji men had been shot, and now Dayne had been hit too. He was struggling to his feet, trying to drag himself and the young man with him toward the trees.

Suddenly Ollie appeared further down the beach and the gunfire began again. It was a diversion. Without thinking about what she was doing, she found herself on the beach with a hand clamped around the downed man's arm, pulling right along with Dayne. Two metres to go. One metre.

The shots ceased. Was the shooter reloading? They reached the trees. Nethania hauled with all her might and dragged Ra-kin out of sight. Dayne staggered after her. She hoped Ollie had ducked out of sight now that they were safe.

She stopped long enough to look into the young man's face and her heart sank. His eyes were wide open and unseeing. He was dead.

"All for the love of money!" She spat the words. She wanted to rail for their stupidity.

What was worse, Dayne had risked his life to rescue a man who had cared only about preserving wealth.

She turned to him now. He had dropped to his knees beside them. Her heart leapt into her throat. His t-shirt was soaked in blood. His glazed eyes met hers and she felt her chest constrict. He was slowly bleeding to death.

Nethania was about to go to him when she heard careful footsteps close by. She froze and her eyes darted toward the sound. Was it Ollie? Or was it one of the armed men? What felt like an interminable length of time passed. It had to be only a matter of seconds.

She glanced at Dayne and moved quietly to his side. She was helping him to his feet when a man stepped from behind a tree. She recognised him instantly.

A sadistic smile curled Garvey's lips and he aimed his rifle at Dayne.

36

Ollie gave a flick of his wrist and released the knife at the precise distance he knew it would take. It whispered through the air with deadly speed and found its mark.

His heart felt cold in his chest, like a block of ice as the man dropped to his knees and then slumped forward. Nethania's shocked gaze flew from the dead man to Ollie who had just stepped into her line of sight.

He felt both regret and relief. He hated to take a life. At the same time, if his aim had been off, his best friend would be dead. He pushed aside what he had just done and forced his mind to keep control.

"There's one more close by. We've got to get out of here." He strode the last few metres and assessed his friend.

Dayne's legs gave out and he took Nethania down with him. Ollie made a grab for his arm and managed to keep him from falling backward into a tree. Dayne landed on his posterior with Nethania still under his arm on the other side. He was conscious, but barely.

Nethania crawled out from under his weight. "We can use his shirt to apply pressure to stop the bleeding."

"Good idea, but we better be quick."

Ollie took the knife from Dayne's waistband and cut

away his friend's t-shirt. When it had been removed, he was able to get a better view of the gunshot wound. Old memories flooded his mind at the sight of the bullet hole in Dayne's left shoulder.

He quickly wadded and packed the t-shirt over the entry site, then realised he had nothing to hold it there. Nethania solved his dilemma by using her own hand.

"I've got it. Help me get him to his feet and I'll keep it in place."

"The rifle." Dayne's words were a hoarse whisper.

"Don't worry, I won't forget. Hang in there buddy." Ollie collected the .223 from the dead man and slung it over his shoulder using the strap attached. He checked the downed man's pockets and found a box of cartridges. He pocketed those. He would have to retrieve the pack from where he had left it fifty metres down the tree line.

He turned to Dayne and found that with Nethania's help, he had made it to his feet. She was under his left arm now, keeping pressure on the wound. Ollie wrapped an arm around his friend's waist and propped himself under Dayne's right.

"This way." Nethania indicated the direction to the overhang with a nod of her head.

~

Bruno knelt beside his mate and felt rage flow

through his veins. Knife, right through the heart. Whoever these men were, they were dangerous. The two Asian men were dead, and according to Trevor, he had hit one of the two Caucasians, not the one they had tied aboard the boat earlier. That left the woman and the one she called Ollie.

They would retreat for now to regroup. And he intended to use that to his advantage. He strode to the beach and gestured for Trevor to join him. His deck hand didn't have the stomach for this kind of task, not like Garvey. But he had surprisingly managed to kill two and wound a third.

His thirst for money clearly outweighed the voice of his conscience. Good. Bruno was counting on it. They had a job to finish. And now it was personal.

~

Dayne was barely conscious when Nethania and Ollie eased him onto the floor of the overhang. To enter, they had climbed over a one metre wall of rock and then into a three metre long by one and a half metre wide space inside. It was defensible, if a little cramped. Nethania supposed it had been created during World War Two. It had the markings of a man made look out.

They leaned Dayne against the back wall and he forced heavy lids open. He scanned the overhang.

"Good spot you picked." He smiled wanly at Nethania.

"How are you feeling?" She checked the bullet hole beneath the blood-soaked cloth and was relieved the flow had stopped.

"Alive." His lids drooped and his head began to dip.

"Stay with us Dayne. Keep talking."

He seemed to force his eyes open and his head up. "Ollie."

Ollie laid the rifle down and removed the pack from his back. "I'm here, mate."

"Sorry I let you down. Thought I could get to Ra-kin first."

Ollie gently wedged the pack behind Dayne to make him more comfortable. "You're one brave hombre, but if you ever do that again, I'll kill you myself."

A weak smile tugged at Dayne's lips and his eyes slid shut. "Wasn't brave. Was scared."

The soft reply was barely above a whisper. Nethania's heart broke, and her only thought was 'wow!' She glanced at Ollie and saw her own feelings reflected in his expression.

The injured man's head rolled forward as he lost consciousness.

"Dayne?" He shook his friend gently.

Nethania checked for a pulse in his carotid artery. "Shallow but steady."

Ollie released a relieved breath. "I never should have suggested we row to Murphy Island."

Nethania placed a hand on his forearm. "You couldn't have known what those men were doing. This is not your fault."

He eased Dayne onto his side and ensured his airway was open. Nethania scooted out of the way in the crowded space. Ollie settled back on the other side of his friend and studied his hands. They were covered in maroon stains and slightly shaky.

"What happened back there? I thought you were taking the Aiji's to this place."

Nethania wiped her bloody hands on her shorts and shook her head in disgust. "They wouldn't go. They were convinced you and Dayne were after the gold too. That's why they returned to the beach. They were going after the treasure."

Ollie smiled mirthlessly and ran his hands through his hair. "What will it profit a man if he gain the whole world, and yet lose his soul?"

Nethania recognised the familiar Scripture from her readings. "I caught up to them and tried to convince them it was a bad idea, but Mr. Aiji was determined. I shrank into the background."

Tears pooled in her vivid blue eyes and she let them flow. She felt the pain God must be feeling. He had just lost two souls for eternity, and all because of greed.

Ollie reached across the space to gently clasp her hand. "You tried to talk sense into them. That's all you could have done." He met and held her gaze, his own radiating gratitude. "Thanks for saving Dayne's life."

"I couldn't have done it without your diversion. And then that man with the gun…" A shudder rippled through her.

She was sad at his lost eternity too. Although guilt-ily grateful he was dead and not them. She had not missed the fact he would have shot Dayne first and saved her for some fun later. It had been in his eyes. She had no idea what to do with what she had seen today.

"How do men get so wholly taken over by evil?" she whispered in dismay.

Ollie gave her hand a squeeze and released it. "Not all at once I would imagine. It takes time and sin to sear a conscience that black."

Her vulnerable gaze met his. "I think I understand what you meant earlier about love being in opposition to evil. Thanks for what you did."

Ollie's grey eyes were a depth of sadness, guilt and knowledge. "I don't feel good having blood on my hands. But I've been around long enough to know someone's gotta oppose what those men stood for, and talk won't cut it."

Nethania read between the lines. "You've killed before?"

"I've used my weapon in self defence. Have I ever killed a man like I did today? No. But I've been on the receiving end of a bullet, and let's just say I know how Dayne's feeling right now."

Moisture clouded her vision. Was it compassion that caused her heart to clench painfully? Or something special about this man that drew her? She didn't analyse it. Couldn't analyse anything. The shakes were taking over and her insides felt like jelly. Her brain was shutting off and her thoughts felt like they were bogged down. This was not how she had imagined her rescue day to end.

37

"We're going to miss you, Teddy."

Amelia smiled at Carrie's use of her nickname. Her friend placed a casserole dish on the table and sat. Paul was to her right and Amelia to her left.

"I'll miss you too. But judging by the email Linc sent, it won't be forever."

Carrie's eyes lit with enjoyment. She never ceased to delight in the romance that was playing out in Amelia's life.

"What did he say?"

Carrie placed a large portion of tuna Casserole on her plate and passed the serving spoon to Amelia. She explained the brief missive while she served herself. She glanced self-consciously at her brother as she concluded, only to find him smiling with satisfaction.

"I think I like this guy the more I hear about him."

Amelia's gaze narrowed. Was he happy for her because Linc was committed, or because he might get his chance for 'the talk' he and Steven had planned? "No warning uppercuts or left hooks!"

"He's navy, grease monkey. I'm not that stupid. I'll leave that stuff to Steven. That doesn't mean I can't play a few pranks though does it?" Paul took a mouthful of food. His eyes gleamed with mischief as he chewed.

Amelia wanted to strangle him. "If you two chase him off, you'll rue the day you were born!"

Carrie chuckled. "I wouldn't worry, Teddy. Something tells me Linc won't be put off easily."

Amelia gave her friend an uncertain glance. If her brothers ruined her one chance for happiness, she would thrash them to within an inch of their lives. Even if they were head and shoulders above her.

"So what time do you leave tomorrow?" Carrie spooned some cheesy tuna and pasta into her mouth and turned to Paul.

He passed Amelia a cheeky glance before becoming serious again. "It'll be a long day. I was hoping to get an early start." He studied his sister. "Is seven am okay?"

Amelia gave him a dry smile. "You forget I've been in the navy for a few years. I'm used to watching the sun come up. Seven will be a sleep in."

"It's settled then." He smiled and took another mouthful.

Carried paused with her spoon in hand. "That's so soon." She looked at Amelia with a regretful light in her caring eyes. "This house will be lonely with you gone."

Amelia's heart clenched. Carrie was quite possibly the best friend she'd ever had. "I'm only a phone call away."

Carrie mustered a grin. "Oh don't you worry. You'll hear from me so often I'll start driving you nuts."

Amelia relaxed. "I'm counting on it."

~

It was dark and the weather was cutting up. Nethania studied Ollie across the small cavern in the dim moonlight. He was rubbing the back of his head. Judging by the pained expression on his face, the knot on his skull was giving him some grief.

"Are you okay?"

At Nethania's soft question, he dropped his hands to his bent knees and smiled ruefully.

"Never better."

She frowned with displeasure. "It's alright to admit you're in pain, Ollie."

"Fine." His sharp tone cut through the tension in the cool night air. "My head is hurting like crazy and I'm worried about Dayne. I hate waiting for them to find us when I could be doing something useful to get us out of here."

Nethania's lips lifted at the corners in an enigmatic smile. She was grateful for his honesty. "That's more like it. What do we do?"

"Dayne needs a hospital. The only way to get help is to either steal some oil for our boat, or take their vessel. The only problem is I don't want to move Dayne."

"We can move him slow and steady together."

"But what if they're still watching the beach?"

Nethania considered his question. He had a valid point. Her gaze drifted to the trees being whipped violently by the inbound storm. "I doubt they'll be out in this weather. They'd be mad to stay onboard their boat. If I was them, I would take cover on the island and wait it out."

Ollie was quiet for several pensive moments. He shifted to face her and his penetrating gaze held hers across the small space.

"If I can find out where they are, we might have a chance."

"You do realise that we might get ourselves shipwrecked in a storm like this. I've been tossed around in a brutal ocean once before and I don't relish the thought of doing it again."

Ollie's anxious gaze dropped to Dayne between them. His breathing was ragged as he slept, due to the immense pain he was in. He hadn't awoken since their arrival. His loss of blood was concerning, and his need for medical attention only heightened with every passing hour. The chance of infection, dehydration and other complications was huge the longer they waited.

"I'll risk it."

Nethania studied Ollie's intense grey eyes and fortified her heart. She had survived a storm tossed sea once. She could do it again. "Me too."

Ollie's shoulders relaxed a little and he exhaled. She realised he must have been holding his breath pending her response. She smiled. He clearly did not want to leave her behind, but also desperately wanted to get his friend to the mainland. The quandary had obviously tied him in knots. She liked his sense of honour.

"How do you intend to find where they are?"

He rose to his knees and retrieved the pack. He secured it on his back and slung the rifle over his shoulder on its strap. "I'll follow the shoreline."

"What if you get into trouble?"

Ollie reached across the space and gripped her hand. "Do *not* come after me. No matter what you hear."

"But-"

"I'll come for you and Dayne. If I'm not back by daylight..."

Nethania read between the lines. "We're on our own."

Turmoil darkened his eyes. "Maybe I should leave you the rifle."

Nethania's lips flattened. "Don't bother. I won't use it."

He opened his mouth, presumably to lecture her. She cut him off with a dry look.

"I've already proven how useless I am when it comes to defending myself with a weapon. It's not that I don't want to use it. It's that I can't."

"When it comes down to it, I'd rather you alive than them. They will kill you and Dayne if they get the chance."

"Well I'll just pray they won't."

Ollie did not look happy about her plan. He shook his head and muttered under his breath as he manoeuvred his way out of the overhang. Nethania watched him go with mounting trepidation.

Papa, we need you big time. Ollie especially. Keep him safe and bring him back soon? Preserve Dayne?

Please help me to be strong? While I was here on the island alone I thought I was tough. Now I see it was a false trust.

In the quiet moments after her prayer, she sensed a calming presence. He was close. She sighed with relief and swiped at unexpected tears.

It was not false trust or false faith, daughter. It was baby steps for a toddler. Now it's time to run.

Nethania smiled. She liked the analogy. She also wondered what it meant for her to have faith enough to move from baby steps to running.

While she was still pondering that thought, Dayne began to stir.

38

Ollie spotted their campsite while he was on his way down the hillside. He could see the glow of a fire close to the shore from his vantage point. He was tempted to save time and simply return for Nethania and Dayne. However, the possibility that only one man might be there was high. He needed to know the whereabouts of both.

He slunk between wind battered trees in the direction of the fire. It took a good twenty minutes. He drew to within fifty metres of the campsite and was quite impressed.

He crouched in the undergrowth and was able to see the remaining men had created cover between two boulders in a rocky outcrop on the border of the beach. They had spread a tarpaulin across them and tied it firmly in place like a roof. In the centre was a campfire crackling along nicely, sheltered from the worst of the wind by the boulders. Palm fronds were spread out and two suspicious forms beneath them indicated that the men were asleep.

Ollie quietly backed away and crept in the direction he had come. It appeared that now was the time to make a break for the boat.

~

Dayne mumbled in his sleep. Nethania listened with intrigue as he stirred. She shifted beside him so that she was able to look properly into his face.

"They're down. Get the kids out! ... Sean, no Sean!" He jerked awake and his hands reached up to shield his face.

Sweat beaded his forehead and trickled into his brown hair. His breathing came hard and in gasps.

Nethania laid a reassuring hand on his shoulder. "Sh, Dayne, you're safe for now, but you need to stay quiet."

His arms lowered. His stricken gaze met hers and focused. He swallowed hard and his breathing settled. Nethania read a world of agony in his brown eyes.

"They died."

Nethania's heart broke over his shattered admission. Dayne squeezed his eyes shut and covered them with his good hand. Still, drops of moisture slipped from behind them. What had this man undergone while in the military that haunted his dreams?

"Who died?"

"Sean and I tried, but the mongrel flicked the switch."

Nethania tried to piece the disjointed information together. Hostages. His comrade Sean. A bad guy and a switch.

A terrorist had detonated a bomb?

"Was this when you were in the military? Did a terrorist blow up a building?"

Dayne nodded ever so slightly.

"Did Sean survive?"

He shook his head. "We only had time to pull out our injured. Sean went back for the kids. We thought we had them all, but there was one left."

A school.

"One child or one terrorist?"

Dayne released a shuddering breath. "Terrorist."

Nethania thought she had a pretty good idea now what had happened. "I'm sorry Dayne."

He wiped his eyes and stared at her as if seeing her for the first time. She doubted he had talked about that incident with others. Ollie might know. But then maybe he didn't.

"It wasn't your fault."

His eyes shuttered and she watched as he visibly closed himself off from his past.

"Don't do that."

At Nethania's sharp command, he blinked and stared at her in surprise.

"Don't shut off. The past will always haunt you until you learn to talk about it."

He closed his eyes and shook his head. "You don't wanna hear about the terrified screams, the blood or the burnt remains of-" His voice broke.

He was right. She didn't. But clearly he needed someone to tell. "Try me." There was steel in her tone and he must have caught it.

An intrigued light flickered in his gaze. He studied her

in silence for a long time.

"They gave me the Victoria Cross." He turned his face to the rock overhang above him, his expression bitter. "I didn't want it. Didn't deserve it. I couldn't save my team or those kids. If I'd done a better sweep after the raid then just maybe I'd have known there was one more hiding."

"Were you leading the mission?"

"No. Sean was."

"Where were the other men in your team? Two isn't enough."

"Two were hit in the raid. I dragged out Tom while Sean hauled Jace. The others were with the kids, checking them over."

"And you were the only survivor."

Dayne took a deep breath and exhaled slowly. His jaw muscles worked as he fought for control. "Tom made it."

Nethania eased her fingers into his large hand and held on. "You weren't the only one who missed the terrorist hiding. Every one of you deserved a medal for trying to help those kids."

He remained silent.

"It was God who spared you, Dayne. Don't be sorry you're alive. I'm not. You saved mine and Ollie's lives today."

He looked at her and offered a smile that did not quite reach his eyes. He gave her hand a squeeze and released it.

That he did not believe her was obvious. Yet Nethania was not put off by his kind dismissal. "I'll be praying God brings healing into your life, in more ways than one."

The smile he offered her next was genuine and she reciprocated.

"You're one special lady Nethania."

She huffed and waved off his compliment. "You're just being nice because I'm your nurse and I might decide to poke around that shoulder if you're not."

He grinned and his eyes slid shut wearily. "You remind me of my mum."

Nethania raised one brow in question. She had been told she reminded others of many people, but never their mother!

"You're stubborn." He shifted an inch to get comfortable and winced.

Her eyes narrowed.

"But with a heart of gold," he mumbled and drifted toward sleep.

Nethania's face eased into a chuffed smile. In its own way, the remark was kind of sweet. She decided right then and there to adopt Dayne. He would make a great addition to her extended family. Not to mention she was a sucker for wounded ducks, so to speak.

She heard movement above the sound of wind in the trees and checked the watch on Dayne's wrist. Forty minutes. It had to be Ollie.

39

Ollie saw a shadow pass through the trees on the hillside above him and his heart nearly stopped in his chest. Sickening realisation struck him square in the gut.

It had been a trick!

Those bodies beneath the fronds hadn't been their hunters. They had laid a trap to catch their prey. Only Ollie hadn't taken the bait. He hadn't closed in for the kill. But he had thought Nethania, Dayne and himself were safe for the time being.

Ollie broke into a run through the forest toward the overhang. He had been dreadfully wrong, and this time it was going to cost his friends' lives.

~

Nethania saw a head peer over the rock wall surrounding the overhang. A rifle barrel followed and her heart leapt into her throat. The moonlit figure stood to full height and emitted a sadistic chuckle.

The space between them was only a metre or so. Without thinking through her actions, she leapt to her feet and grabbed for the weapon. Her fingers found the rifle stock and pushed at the same time a deafening boom challenged the stormy gale for volume.

A bullet pinged off the rock behind her and whooshed past her left ear. There was the horrible sound of a thud and a grunt as it found flesh. The shadowed figure stumbled backward and fell.

Nethania dropped to the ground out of sight. She glanced at Dayne. He was trying to rise. She crawled to his side and pushed him back down.

"His own bullet hit him," she whispered.

"Is he dead?"

"I'll check."

"No. I'll go."

"Sorry soldier. It's my turn to fight the good fight. Stay put. Nurse's orders."

Dayne did not look one bit pleased. He also barely had enough strength to rise onto an elbow let alone walk unassisted. Nethania patted his chest gently and crept to the rock barrier. She peeked over the top.

Another dark figure was crouched beside the downed man. She dropped out of sight with her back to the wall. Her heart was pounding loudly in her ears and panic clawed to the surface.

Papa, there's another one. Protect us please?

"Nethania? Dayne?"

At Ollie's soft call, Nethania released the breath she had been holding and her vision clouded with tears of relief.

Thank You God!

"Ollie, we're okay. Is he dead?"

One leg and then another stepped over the barrier and Ollie sank down beside her. "Yes."

Nethania wrapped her arms around her midsection, but what she really wanted was for Ollie's arms to come around her. His kind gaze found hers.

"Are you alright?"

"He appeared out of nowhere and aimed at us. I pushed his gun away and the bullet ricocheted. It missed me and got him."

Ollie's eyes closed in relief and he rested his head against the rock at his back. Nethania watched him gather his composure and was touched by how much he cared.

Definitely something special about this man, Papa.

She touched his arm. "What about you?"

He pushed away from the rock and moved to Dayne's side. His friend was regarding him with eyes filled with questions.

"I found what I thought was their campsite. It looked like they were both asleep by a fire, but it was a trap. I'll bet the other one is still watching it in case we come after them. After that shot, he'll probably head for our position. We've got to leave."

Dayne struggled onto his good elbow and Ollie helped him the rest of the way to his feet. Nethania tucked herself against his bad side and checked the wound. Thankfully the movement had not started him bleeding again.

Wordlessly, they worked together to get Dayne out

of the overhang. He was weak and unsteady, suggest-
ing his loss of blood had been severe.

"Alright buddy." Ollie stepped around the skipper.
"Let's take it slow and careful." He started them down
the hill.

Nethania glanced at him on the other side of their
patient. "What's the plan?"

"Take the boat that still runs."

Nethania's mouth tipped in a lopsided smile. "Got
it."

~

Linc awoke from the nightmare with a gasp and
sprang upright. He instantly regretted the action when
his head collided with the bunk above him. He sank
back onto his mattress and rubbed the sore spot which
was no doubt starting to swell already.

The images from his dream continued to flash before
his mind's eye with startling clarity. The two men were
familiar, but he couldn't place his finger on why. One
was injured and being helped through jungle by the
other and a woman. She had rich caramel skin, long
dark hair pulled into a ponytail and startling blue eyes.
What disturbed him most was an intense feeling of
danger.

He rolled over and tried to shake off the strange
dream. He closed his eyes and sleep tugged at his
thoughts. The dream started to return.

Linc forced heavy lids open and swung his legs to the floor. Evidently good sleep was not going to happen tonight. He needed a change of scenery to shake off the lingering impression the nightmare had left. Terror. That was what he felt.

He was overtired. He had to be. Or maybe he'd eaten too much of Tommo's pizza before bed.

Linc pulled on a pair of uniform pants and a clean grey shirt. He wandered barefoot from his quarters to the galley for a brew. Maybe Tommo still had some hot chocolate left. Amelia liked it. Just the thought of her brought a smile to his face and a lift to his heart.

He entered the galley and found he was not the only one with a brew on the brain. Joshua was making himself a coffee.

"Morning sir."

"Couldn't sleep Linc?"

He yawned. "Bad dream. You?"

"Bad feeling." Joshua leant against the counter and sipped his coffee.

Linc's brows lowered. "What about?"

"A friend. I don't think you've met him, although you'd know who he is. Ollie Startori."

Linc was reaching for a mug in the cupboard and froze. The face and the name clicked into place. He had seen the occupants of The Dream Catcher through binoculars from the bridge. He turned to his boss.

"Okay, this is weird."

Joshua frowned. "Why?"

"I just had a dream about him and his first mate. I

remember them from the day we took those refugee bodies off his boat. I saw Ollie and... what was the other guy's name?"

"Dayne."

"Right. Dayne was injured and Ollie was helping him through a jungle. A woman was with them. I might have seen her somewhere too."

Joshua calmly sipped his coffee and pondered Linc's dream. "What did she look like?"

Linc described her. Joshua's frown deepened.

"Sounds like the picture we were sent of that lady lost at sea over a month ago. I remember her only because of her unusual eyes." Joshua studied his friend pensively.

Linc felt uneasy. That strange impression of danger refused to lift. "Do you think there's something to it? I mean, my dream of them being in danger and your bad feeling?" No sooner had the words left his lips than Linc felt like an idiot. He had never put stock in dreams or superstition.

"I've had these feelings regarding people I know before, and it always turns out something was going on in their lives. I've learned to listen when God prompts me to pray."

That concept was new. "Does God do stuff like that?"

Joshua smiled. "He does. He's also been known to give dreams. The Bible says so."

Linc's expression registered the surprise he felt. "What am I supposed to do?"

"Just what you did. Tell me. Your dream is confirmation in my mind that something is wrong with Ollie." Joshua drained the last of his mug and placed it in the sink. "I'm going to make a few calls."

Linc offered a half hearted wave in acknowledgement. He was baffled. As quickly as the sense of danger had arrived, it lifted.

This is weird, Jesus.

He shook his head and set about making a hot chocolate. He needed sleep and hopefully it would do the trick.

40

"What if he's watching the beach?" Nethania voiced the concern uppermost in her mind.

Judging by the pensive expression on Ollie's face, and the way he nervously ran his tongue along his lower lip as he studied the moonlit sand stretching to a turbulent ocean, it was on his too. His gaze swept the beach to their left and right.

"I'm hoping the darkness will make us harder targets to hit if he is."

Nethania's already pounding heart ramped up several more notches. She glanced at Dayne leaning against a tree beside her, breathing heavily and looking like he was going to pass out. His shoulder had a fresh slow trickle. She was worried. He didn't have a lot of blood left to lose.

Ollie shed the pack and placed an arm around Dayne. Nethania wordlessly took up her position of the last half hour on his wounded side. He groaned softly and his head rolled forward. His body started to go limp.

Ollie gave him a shake. "Stay with us a bit longer buddy."

Dayne pulled himself from a black abyss and blinked owlishly. "Just leave me here. I'll only hold you back."

His words were slightly slurred.

Nethania gave him a gentle squeeze. "Not happening soldier. We're not leaving a man behind."

Ollie gave her an appreciative glance. Dayne managed a small smile until they started moving and his face contorted with silent pain. Ollie paused on the edge of the jungle. Suddenly all light evaporated from the sky.

"The moon's gone behind a cloud. Let's go now!" Ollie hissed.

The dash to the surf practically dragging Dayne was the longest of Nethania's life. Their feet found cold water and they waded deeper and deeper until breakers began crashing over their heads. Nethania fought for each breath.

She was a strong swimmer, and Ollie appeared to be too. However, keeping Dayne's head above the water was possibly the most difficult thing Nethania had ever had to do. She turned onto her back and helped Ollie flip Dayne. He coughed and spluttered, a good sign he was still conscious.

With Dayne between them, they kicked in the direction of the fishing vessel. They passed the breakers. The water was terribly choppy, but thankfully less violent than the surf.

Nethania worried the blood on their clothing and the small amount still seeping from Dayne's shoulder would draw sharks. The threat of gunfire concerned her more. With her heart in her throat, she prayed with every kick of her legs and stroke of her free arm.

A bobbing shadow loomed ahead. She could see the silhouette of the fishing boat. Ollie directed them to the stern. Nethania grasped the edge of the fishing vessel and readjusted Dayne so that her arm was around his collar bone. Ollie climbed aboard.

His arms wordlessly reached down and he managed to get hold of an arm. He pulled, gained a better grip of Dayne's torso, and the injured man disappeared over the rail.

Nethania heard an ominous thud and an exclamation. It sounded like Ollie. Had the other man come back to the boat when he heard the shot?

"You got Bruno, didn't you, you mongrel?"

Nethania's blood ran cold. He had Ollie and Dayne. She swam around the boat and managed to pull herself up on the port side of the wheelhouse. The amount of bobbing the boat was doing due to the nasty weather made it easy to grab the thin rail. She quietly boarded and slunk around the wheelhouse wall. She peered into the darkness as the moon finally came from behind a bank of stormy black clouds.

She recognised the man edging around Ollie who was lying on the deck. Outlined in his hand was a revolver. Ollie was trying to rise.

"I've already killed two men over that gold below. D'you think I'd let you just sail off with it? I'm past the point of no return."

Nethania watched as he peered over the stern rail, obviously looking for her.

"Where is she? Did Bruno get 'er?"

Fear threatened to paralyse her. The knowledge Ollie and Dayne were seconds away from a fatal bullet forced her leaden feet to move.

She charged their attacker at full speed. Despite her balance being affected by the movement of the deck beneath her, their bodies collided. He yelped in surprise and his weapon misfired. An instant later they both toppled over the rail into the roiling sea.

Panicked hands grabbed at Nethania. The shooter was madly trying to climb her to get to the surface. She had no chance. If she couldn't break free, she was going to drown.

Her lungs screamed for oxygen. Terror threatened to overtake her. Suddenly he let go and another hand grabbed her. She was hauled unceremoniously to the surface where she gasped for breath.

Ollie grabbed onto the edge of the boat with one hand and held onto her with the other. She blinked to clear her vision and could see her attacker splashing madly several metres away. Another wave tugged him further from the vessel. The current was carrying him away and he didn't appear to be a strong swimmer.

Ollie pulled himself onto the boat with considerably less energy than before. Where had he been struck? Was he okay? Nethania followed him over the rail and sank onto the deck to catch her breath.

Ollie staggered to the wheelhouse. Minutes later Nethania heard the engine burble to life. Apparently they were leaving the gunman behind. She didn't feel good about it. But considering how he had almost taken their lives and would do so in a heartbeat if he could, she wasn't going to object.

~

With the transfer of the refugees to the Oceanic Viking complete, Joshua turned to the navigator.

"Adjust our heading, Shep, to take us toward this small cluster of islands off the mainland near Cairns." He pointed to the grouping on the chart table in the bridge.

Ben Shepparton studied the map, already performing mental calculations. He called out new coordinates to the helmsman. When the helmsman adjusted their heading, Shep turned to Joshua.

"Why so far south sir? I thought we were tasked to patrol the Arafura for most of this tour."

Joshua took his seat in the captain's chair and Shep returned to his station adjacent.

"We were. Our detour to drop off the refugees took us further south than expected. The Childers is north of us and will take over. We're closer now to the search area being plotted to locate a missing craft."

Shep's curious gaze studied Joshua's guarded features. "What craft sir?"

Joshua drew a deep breath. He knew this news would affect his crew and did not relish delivering it. His pause drew the helmsman, radio operator and engineer's attention.

"The Dream Catcher. Dayne Kovacs was scheduled to meet his parents for a family dinner. They alerted the authorities that his boat was due in around six pm last night and hasn't returned."

There was silence on the bridge as this news was digested.

"Ollie's boat." Shep glanced at the radar screen. "Is the coast guard searching?"

"They began a search an hour ago. So far no luck."

Rain pelted the windshield on the patrol boat. It was a sign of things to come. Lightning illuminated a nasty storm ahead, into which they were now directly sailing.

Joshua continued his silent prayer vigil for Ollie and Dayne. His earlier feeling of disquiet had intensified after his phone calls confirmed Ollie's charter was missing. This was looking to be a long, rough night.

41

Nethania checked Dayne's breathing again. Shallow but steady. She braced her foot against the cupboard to her right. With her back to the closed wheelhouse door, she kept a steadying hand on his good shoulder to keep him in the recovery position.

He was still unconscious, and had been since he was dragged aboard over an hour ago. He was lying on the floor on a long bench cushion. She had done the best she could to bandage his shoulder. Thankfully the cold water had helped to stem the bleeding. He was wrapped now in a warm blanket.

Nethania studied Ollie at the helm in the skipper's chair. The tumultuous sea was buffeting the vessel with a vengeance. So far he had managed to keep it afloat, despite clear signs of a concussion. Memories of another night such as this plagued Nethania's anxious mind and she fought to maintain her trust that God was taking care of them.

Ollie met her gaze. His apprehensive eyes drifted to his friend and then back to her. "I'm sorry we couldn't wait this out in a cove somewhere on Murphy. The fact Dayne can't be roused scares me."

"It's okay. I know we need to head to the mainland. You're doing the right thing."

He held her gaze. His grey eyes communicated appreciation for her support. Nethania wasn't feeling as brave as she sounded.

"Any luck with the radio?"

"No. I think it's been disabled."

Nethania shook her head. "Those guys really didn't want word of what they were up to getting out."

"Would you if you'd just killed two men and attempted murder on three other people?"

"The love of money is the root of all evil."

Ollie's mouth lifted in a half smile. "You got that right."

Silence settled in the wheelhouse again. Although it could hardly be termed quiet with the noise of the slashing rain and raging waters outside.

Nethania's favourite hymn came to mind and she automatically began singing it. The words soothed her spirit and bolstered her courage.

"'When peace like a river attendeth my way,
When Sorrows like sea billows roll;
Whatever my lot, Thou has taught me to say,
It is well, it is well with my soul...'"

Nethania was pleasantly surprised when Ollie joined her. His voice was a mellow baritone. Another asset she added to her list of things she liked about him.

A nasty wave collected the vessel from side on and spun it ninety degrees. Ollie muttered under his breath as he fought to correct their course. Nethania squeezed her eyes shut and prayed.

"We're too heavy. This is going to keep happening if

we don't lighten the load. We just don't have the ma-
neuverability we need."

Nethania's eyes opened and studied his profile. "We
can toss the gold."

He met her gaze, his own regretful. "I'll tie the wheel
to keep us straight, then we'll drag it up and dump it
over the edge."

Nethania didn't care what happened to it, just as
long as they survived. "I'll wedge a couple of pillows to
keep Dayne in one place so he doesn't roll around."

They set to work. In minutes they were heading to
the hold where several crates and eskies were bulging
with glittering treasures. They hesitated for only a moment before working together to drag it topside.

Ollie paused at the GPS on their way through the
wheelhouse for the last time.

"Are we doing alright?"

He looked at her in surprise. "Yeah, still on course.
Barely. The sooner we turf this overboard, the better."

They continued dragging the loot onto the deck. Ollie secured a rope around both himself and Nethania
and tied it to the rail for safety. Then together they
hefted the treasure over the edge. With a large splash,
each sank like a stone beneath the waves.

The lashing rain chased them back into the wheelhouse for cover. Ollie untied their rope and also the
wheel and took control. Nethania went in search of a
couple more blankets. She wove unsteadily with the
pitching of the boat back to the wheelhouse with one
around herself. The other she draped over Ollie's soak-

ing wet t-shirt.

He gripped the hand on his shoulder and held her gaze. A mixture of gratitude and anxiety pooled in their depths. "Thanks. Will you find the life vests?"

She knew what that meant and her heart plummeted.

Not again! Please Papa, not again?

Instead of succumbing to the tears she felt, she clenched her teeth, took a deep breath and nodded. He gave her hand a final squeeze before releasing her. His intense focus returned to the stormy sea outside and she went to find the life jackets, all the while praying they wouldn't be needed.

~

"Sir, I'm picking up a contact on radar. It's signature is indicating it's The Bier Man, an Australian fishing vessel."

"Interesting name." Joshua smiled in amusement. "Jaffa, see if you can make contact."

"Yes sir."

Jaffa's voice was the only one heard on the bridge, followed by static. "No response. Want me to keep trying sir?"

"Yes."

Jaffa's repeated failed attempts at communication aroused Joshua's suspicion. Maybe Ollie's boat wasn't the only one in trouble in this storm.

"Shep, is the vessel within the target range the coastguard supplied?"

"Yes sir."

"Alright, adjust our heading and let's check it out."

"Yes sir."

42

Another wave buffeted the fishing vessel and turned it parallel to the storm. Ollie worked the wheel with determination. Another wave collided with the port side and the boat tilted.

"I think we're going to capsize!"

Ollie's urgent warning twisted Nethania's stomach in knots. "We can't! Dayne would never make it to the surface while unconscious. You have to fight it!"

Ollie's intent gaze remained focused on the water outside trying to kill them. His hands spun the wheel against the current. He almost had the bow heading into the wind when another wave broadsided them. The force rolled the vessel forty-five degrees.

Nethania did her best to keep Dayne in a safe position. Meanwhile, her heart was in her throat. She watched Ollie turn the wheel this way and that trying to right it. Finally he had it back into the weather, slicing through huge swells.

"Praise God! The cavalry's here!"

Nethania rose onto unsteady feet and peered out the windshield. A light appeared ahead through the darkness.

"Another boat?"

Lightning strafed the sky. Ollie grinned.

"I'd know that silhouette anywhere. It's an Armidale patrol boat."

"What's that?"

Ollie sent her a sideways grin that managed to warm her to her toes. "A navy warship."

Nethania let loose a whoop of delight. Her joy see-sawed quickly to anxiety. "Will they see us?"

"We'll be on their radar. I'm guessing they've tried to make radio contact and because we haven't answered, they're checking us out."

The boat pitched and Nethania lost her balance. She fell backward into the bare bench seat and then onto the floor beside Dayne, landing almost on top of him. Her thigh sent out a sharp protest and she gritted her teeth against the pain. She would have a nasty bruise by morning.

"You okay?"

Nethania braced herself with a foot on the cupboard, another on the doorframe before her, and her back to the wall. "Fantastic if that ship is headed our way."

Ollie spun the wheel again and increased power to scale a large swell. He managed it fairly well and the vessel slid down into a dip. Another wave reared its head and he repeated the process.

The light in the distance drew nearer.

"How will they get us on board? How will they even communicate if our radio is down?"

"They'll likely send a RHIB over."

"What's a RHIB?"

"Rigid Hulled Inflatable Boat. And don't worry, it's designed to handle rough weather. It's pretty hard to sink one."

Nethania absorbed the information and felt hope buoy her spirit. Another ten minutes of bouncing around on the ocean like a rubber ducky in a bathtub did nothing to ease her nauseated stomach.

"They're here, on our starboard side."

Nethania gingerly stood and peered out the window. She could not see much. Another burst of lightning illuminated a large shadow roughly sixty metres away sailing parallel. Her heart leapt for joy. Within minutes she heard a loud speaker over the roar of the storm. She opened the wheelhouse door to hear.

"Vessel on my port side, this is Australian Warship HMAS Hartfield..."

The rest of what was said was masked by a huge clap of thunder.

"You hold us steady, Ollie. I'm going to wave at them for help."

Ollie's alarmed gaze swung to her. "You watch out for side wash. A rogue wave could dump you in the sea on a night like this."

"I'll hold onto something." Nethania grasped the doorframe and waved one arm madly.

~

Linc focused his binoculars and studied the scene

279

upon the fishing vessel. Light from the wheelhouse spilled onto the deck and he was able to see a dark skinned woman waving in the doorway. He recognised her immediately, from her pony tail right down to what she was wearing. He was gobsmacked.

He lowered the binoculars and stared at Joshua in astonishment. "It's them. It's the people from my dream."

Joshua did not look altogether surprised at his whispered observation, but then he was the one who had passed Linc the binoculars. He placed a reassuring hand on Linc's shoulder.

"It was God after all, hey Lieutenant."

Linc let out a long breath. "Seems so sir."

"Prepare a boarding party and tell Farmer we'll need him on the RHIB. Just between the two of us, if your dream is any indication, Dayne may be on board and in need of medical attention. I'll have Jamie prep the wardroom."

"Yes sir."

Still reeling from shock, Linc quietly descended from the bridge to suit up for a rough ride. Orders followed him on the ship's intercom and crew scattered to fulfil them.

~

Ollie had been right. She marvelled as another wave washed over both the deck of the fishing boat and the

RHIB. The inflatable, although jostled by the tumultu-ous water, remained fairly steady. It's crew was taking Dayne on board.

They placed him in a seat and positioned one sailor on either side to keep him stable and his airway open. Ollie, who had helped transfer his friend, was pulled on board next.

He gripped a rail on one of the seat backs. With one of his feet in the RHIB and another on the inflated rim, he reached for Nethania. She moved closer to the stern of the fishing boat. Behind her was the last navy sailor. He had introduced himself earlier as the executive of-ficer.

Without anyone at the helm, the boat was suffering the full effect of the storm. It bobbed and rocked wildly from side to side. Nethania was reaching for Ollie's hand when there was a shout. She glanced over her shoulder to see the executive officer waving his men off. The RHIB obediently backed away.

Nethania's confusion disappeared when she felt the deck pitch to the side and keep tilting. She felt the wash of the wave tumbling over them even as her feet slipped out from under her and she crashed into the side rail. A solid hand grabbed her around the waist and hung on.

She took a deep breath a split second before the deck was suddenly coming down on top of them. She registered pain. In the chaos she could not pin point what was hurting. Neither could she orient herself in the churning blackness of the ocean around her. Her life vest wanted to pull her to the surface, instead it glued her to the capsized vessel above her.

Only there was no air pocket.

Feeling dazed and disoriented, she struggled to free herself. Her lungs screamed for air. Competent hands pushed her fumbling attempts aside and unzipped the vest. She struggled out of it.

The officer clamped a powerful forearm around her collar bone and swam down and then up. On her way to the surface, Nethania saw an aura surround the hull of the inflatable. A spotlight?

She tried to kick. However, it was the sailor that propelled her upward. Their heads broke the surface and they gasped for breath. Nethania told her limbs to swim to the RHIB a couple of metres away. Yet she couldn't seem to coordinate them. What was wrong?

She could see the outline of men on the inflatable and a wash of light. Yet it didn't make any sense. Every image danced together in a strange blur. Another wave washed over their heads.

Voices shouted and hands reached down. She could feel herself being plucked from the depths, but all as though from another world.

"Is she okay?"

"She's bleeding."

"Get the X!"

Bleeding? Nethania struggled to focus. She was being held upright in one of the seats in the front of the RHIB. A firm arm held her securely around the waist and pressed against a solid chest. She located the source of the pain and gingerly fingered the side of her head. Something warm flowed over her fingertips.

"Got him. Coz, get us out of here."

A large hand pressed upon the sore spot on her skull. She winced and tried to push it aside.

"Hold still Nethania. I'm just trying to stop the bleeding."

Ollie's voice. She ceased struggling.

"Alright is Dayne?" She frowned. That wasn't the order she had intended her words to come out, and they were slurred.

"He's okay. We all are. Hang in there and soon we'll be on board with a hot cup of coffee and some dry clothes."

The arm around her tightened momentarily to punctuate the encouragement. Ollie had her. She relaxed. Everything was going to be alright.

43

"Nethania Brideson, you have no idea what an en-couragement it's been to the crew to find you. The coast guard and navy gave up on you a month ago."

Nethania glanced up into a pair of smiling blue eyes, set in a handsome face and framed by short, dark hair. The room was still swimming a little. She couldn't be sure if it was the ocean tossing the patrol boat around, or the concussion from the knock she had taken when the fishing vessel capsized.

"Well, God certainly didn't." She smiled and offered her hand. She tried to stand but just couldn't manage it.

The officer waved her back down onto the bench seat and took the hand she offered.

She was in what they called the wardroom. The table had been converted into a bed for Dayne. Nearby, the coxswain, a kind red head they all called Farmer, was keeping a close eye on the patient from a chair beside the 'bed'.

Dayne had an IV dripping fluids into his bloodstream and an oxygen mask covering his mouth and nose. He had been pumped full of painkillers and was rest-ing peacefully. His pulse, although shallow, remained steady.

"You must be the captain." Nethania held the sore patch on her head, which had been padded and bandaged as soon as she arrived on board.

The shower she had taken, although short and bumpy in the choppy sea, had been heavenly. She was now in a fresh two-piece disruptive pattern navy uniform. It was apparently fire retardant and used for operations, training activities, general dirty work and for boarding. She was learning a few things.

"Yes. Lieutenant Commander Joshua Donnelly." He leaned against the sink in the corner for balance, only a stride or two away.

So the ship was indeed still pitching. At least it wasn't all in her head.

"Ollie briefed me on what happened. It's a remarkable story."

Nethania smiled dryly. "One I'll be happy to forget."

"I can imagine. Are you hungry?"

Nethania stared at the captain as though he had lost his mind. Her stomach was rolling right along with the room.

He laughed. "I get the picture. I just dropped by to let you know we'll be in port within the hour. The federal police will meet you. An ambulance will be there to take Dayne to the hospital. Perhaps we should ask for two?"

Nethania waved her hand in dismissal. "I'll be fine when my feet touch down on solid ground."

Joshua Donnelly chuckled. "Alright. Until then, if there's anything you need, just let someone know."

Nethania smiled appreciatively. "You've already done more than enough. I'm extremely grateful. Oh, and please tell your executive officer I'm thankful for what he did."

Joshua smiled. "I will, and you're welcome. Rest up. I'll see you topside soon."

Nethania returned his smile and waved as he exited. As he left, Ollie entered. Her smile widened. He looked much better. He had showered and shaved and his equilibrium seemed to have returned. Although appearing to be tired, his eyes were clear.

"Catching up with your old crew?"

He smiled. "Some of them anyway. A lot have moved on." He glanced at Farmer and nodded toward Dayne. "How is he?"

"Stable for now. He'll need surgery when we reach port, so he's not out of the woods yet."

Ollie studied his unconscious friend with concern. "He's tough. He'll pull through."

He turned his attention on Nethania and she could have sworn she saw his gaze soften.

"How are you feeling?"

"I know how you felt yesterday and again last night. I should have been more sympathetic."

Ollie's eyes took on a warm glow. "I don't know about that. I thought you were pretty understanding. And you did save our necks a couple of times."

Nethania smiled and dropped her gaze to the table. She wanted to sleep. "That goes both ways."

"Move over. I'll keep you company."

Nethania glanced up in surprise. She shuffled along the bench and Ollie sat beside her.

"Thanks."

He sent her a toe curling smile. "Not much of a hardship if you ask me."

Nethania's cheeks warmed. Was he flirting with her? She smiled back. She certainly hoped so.

She had not been expecting him to walk into her life. She was holding onto a hope that he wouldn't just walk out. She wanted a chance to get to know him better in more stable circumstances. Although she liked what she had seen so far.

When pushed to the brink, he had exhibited a caring and faithful nature. His faith ran deep. She liked that. In fact, there wasn't much she didn't like. Those grey eyes and that smile had a way of sending tingles through her. She'd never experienced this kind of attraction before. Infatuation was one thing. This was another.

She glanced at Farmer. He was staring at the two of them with a knowing gleam in his smiling eyes. Ollie ignored him and stretched his legs, folded his hands across his chest and let his head fall back against the seat. A contented smile settled around the corners of his mouth.

Nethania resisted a smile herself and laid her head on the edge of Dayne's 'bed'. Although disturbed by nausea and a nasty headache, she tried to catch some rest. She doubted she would get another chance once they disembarked.

~

Nethania was more surprised than ever when her parents met her on the dock in Cairns. She was enfolded by two pairs of arms. Her mother, who was shorter than her by at least a foot, with dark skin and long jet black hair, wept. Her father, a white Australian with fair hair and light blue eyes, was in tears as well.

They held each other for a long time and then the conversation began to flow in a jumble of languages with exclamations of delight and questions. Nethania answered her mother in Sinhala and her father in English.

Nethania caught sight of Ollie climbing into an ambulance nearby beside Dayne. Sadness tightened her chest. She hadn't had a chance to get his number.

As the rear door closed, she met his gaze for a brief moment. He offered a small wave. She returned it, disappointed that their friendship had ended as quickly as it had begun.

She returned her attention to her parents, although part of her wilted with the departure of the emergency vehicle.

44

Nethania pushed through the swinging door to the medical ward two days later and stopped at the desk to inquire which direction to Dayne Kovacs' room. Finally assured she was heading the right way, she found his door open and walked tentatively inside.

An older couple was sitting one either side of his bed. The gentleman was an older version of Dayne, with white hair and intuitive brown eyes. A short, cuddly woman with blond hair curled around her face sat on the other side. His parents?

They noticed her and rose. The man approached her with a huge smile and grasped her hand between his in a warm hold. He shook it while speaking.

"You must be Netania."

His accent reminded her of the Count from Sesame Street.

"Dayne has told us all about you."

Nethania was stunned by the warm reception. The woman brushed her husband aside to hug her.

"Our son told us how you saved his life. We are so grateful." She held Nethania at arm's length, her gaze teary.

Nethania smiled. "He saved mine too. Did he tell you that?"

She shrugged and smiled. "Zat is our Dayne. It is not surprising. Come, sit."

Before Nethania could object, she was ushered into the gentleman's chair by the window. Dayne stirred and she forgot all about his parents.

He looked pale. Thankfully all that was attached to him was a drip. Obviously he was out of danger. His brown eyes focused on his mum at the foot of the bed and he smiled.

Nethania was intrigued when he greeted her in another language. She responded in kind and indicated their guest. Dayne shifted his head on the pillow to see her. She met his gaze and offered a smile.

"Hi soldier. How are you doing?"

His mouth eased into a grin. "Pretty good. They're letting me out of this prison in a couple of days." His eyes sparkled mischievously. "Ollie is going to be jealous."

"What do you mean?"

Dayne smiled broadly. "He's been trying to chase up your number and address for the last forty-eight hours and is kicking himself he forgot to ask you before we all left the ship."

Nethania could not restrain her delighted smile. "Really?"

"I'll rub it in that I saw you first."

Nethania laughed. "I wouldn't stress too much if I was him. You two are stuck with me now."

Dayne chuckled, coughed and then winced. He drew a deep breath and then looked at her steadily. "Thanks, for everything."

"I owe you my life too, Dayne. We're even."

"Well I'm going to owe you again if you'll rustle up some Macca's or Hungry Jacks for me. The food in here is terrible."

Nethania glanced at his parents. His mother was wagging a finger at him and his father just shook his head.

She launched off in what sounded like Hungarian. Dayne ignored her reprimand and looked at Nethania with pleading eyes.

"Please?"

Nethania stifled a laugh. "I don't want to get in trouble with your mum."

Dayne winked. "She's just a big pussy cat."

A deep throaty laugh caused Nethania to smile up at Dayne's father. He was enjoying the interchange immensely by the look of it.

"I'll tame da pussy cat if you'll get some for me too," he encouraged.

Dayne's mother turned on him next. Nethania caught the word 'cholesterol' mingled in with the onslaught of Hungarian.

Nethania's sparkling gaze rested on Dayne's mother. "What would you like Mrs. Kovacs?"

The older woman sent her men a final cross glare and then she sighed. Her features eased into a warm smile for Nethania.

"Ice cream please."

Nethania beamed and strode from the room on a

mission.

~

"Hi stranger."

Nethania spun in her church pew to stare wide eyed at Ollie standing beside her in the centre aisle. Nethania's parents exchanged knowing smiles and moved over to allow extra room. He slid in next to her.

"How did you know I'd be here?"

He leaned close and lowered his voice. "A tattle tale in a hospital bed gave me a tip off."

Nethania laughed softly. "I'll deal with him later. How are you going?"

"I'll be a whole lot better if you agree to come to lunch with me after church."

Nethania assessed those grey eyes and found warmth and interest radiating from their depths. A thrill of pleasure rippled through her.

"We're eating at my folks'. You want to come?"

Ollie peered around her at her parents and smiled a greeting. "Would you mind an interloper at lunch?"

Nethania's mum looked like she would burst. "Yes yes, you must come. I feed you curry. You like."

Her father grinned and stretched forth his hand. Ollie shook it.

"The man who brought our daughter home to us will always be welcome at our table."

Ollie looked touched by the comment and nodded

his thanks. Nethania relaxed. Her family's warm reception was a positive sign. She chanced a glance at Ollie and found him grinning at her. She returned it and rose with the rest of the congregation for the opening song.

~

When Linc stepped off the plane in Melbourne, he was blindsided by the flying hug he received from Amelia. He wrapped her in his arms, inhaling the sweet scent that was entirely her own.

"I missed you Teddy!" He buried his face in her hair. It was out and around her shoulders in a riot of cute curls. She was even more lovely than he remembered.

She finally stepped back and looked up into his face with a huge smile. "I missed you too. I started to worry you might change your mind."

His eyes lit with warmth and a great deal of desire. "Not going to happen."

Suddenly she frowned. "Where's Yasmin?"

He smiled and stepped aside. Jaclyn was behind him in the waiting area outside their gate. In her arms was a small pink bundle. Jackie beamed.

"She's here, and she brought her aunty."

Amelia laughed and embraced her sister-in-law-to-be. She then studied the infant with her tiny button nose and a mouth shaped like cupid's bow. She was wearing a small pink dress with smocking and delicate rosebuds.

Amelia sighed and smiled with delight. She reached for the baby. As she did, the infant smiled back and stretched out her arms for a cuddle. Amelia's heart melted.

"What a sweetie!" She snuggled her close and managed to coax several more smiles from the child before she remembered she had company. "Oh sorry!"

Linc was grinning at her and Jaclyn was smiling contentedly. Amelia's cheeks flamed red and she averted her sheepish gaze, nodding in the direction they were to walk.

"We'll collect your baggage."

Linc draped an arm around her shoulder and Jaclyn fell in step on her other side.

"You haven't told me how you're doing." He studied her closely, seeming to note the careful way she moved.

"I'm well. Although I may commit a homicide this week if my brothers do what they're planning to do."

"Which is what?"

"The Jones family hazing."

"As long as I get to be with you, let 'em at it."

Linc's warm smile sent tingles down her spine.

~

An hour and a half later they arrived in Heyworth. Linc had enjoyed the journey. That Amelia's protective family had allowed her to drive alone spoke volumes about her recovery. He was pleased she was doing so well.

Her parents met them in the front yard of a small, country cottage. Several children of various ages raced past in what appeared to be a game of tag. Linc was bombarded with greeting hugs and Jaclyn was then swarmed by three women fawning over the baby. The older of the three ladies had been introduced to them as Amelia's mother. She had been the first to hug him. The other two were her sisters-in-law.

A tall man with salt and pepper hair and a kind, weathered face stepped forward to shake Linc's hand. His brown eyes crinkled at the corners as he smiled.

"It's great to finally meet you, Linc. Amelia speaks highly of you."

Linc responded with a genuine smile despite the butterflies in his stomach. "Thank you sir."

"No need to sir me. Just John will do."

"Yes sir... I mean John."

The older man's eyes took on a cheeky gleam. "Kind o' hard to get the navy out o' ya, isn't it?"

Linc chuckled and lifted a shoulder in a shrug. "It's a way of life."

"Amelia's the same. Come on in." He turned and led the way down a paved footpath framed by rose bushes toward the small cream cottage.

"I'll just bring in some bags. The baby will need some things."

John excused him with a wave.

Amelia took Jaclyn by the arm and escorted her inside. Yasmin had been commandeered by Amelia's mother, Gwen, who was close behind. Her daughters-in-law trailed her talking and laughing.

Linc watched them all with a small amount of awe. They were clearly a close, loving family, something he had always longed to have. He took a moment to thank God for them and grabbed Yasmin's small suitcase and baby bag from the boot of the car.

He wondered absently as he traversed the footpath, where Amelia's two brothers were, Steven and Paul. He could hear their children's raucous shouts from the backyard.

Linc stepped onto the porch and the door opened for him. A young man around six feet tall held it for him to enter. He looked a lot like Amelia, with his brown hair and hazel eyes and freckled nose. However, there the similarities ended. He had broad shoulders and a muscular physique, which his blue jeans and flannel shirt could not hide.

Linc smiled in greeting. "Hi, I'm Linc."

"Paul."

Suddenly a fist came from nowhere and collected Linc in the stomach. He grunted and doubled over, dropping the bags. Before he knew what was happening, he was body slammed and pinned face to the floor with an elbow against his neck.

"This is Steven." Paul's even tone told Linc he knew about the ambush.

"Interesting way to introduce yourselves," Linc managed a calm voice, albeit somewhat muffled by the fact his face was smashed against the carpet in the front entrance.

Steven's deep voice sounded near his ear. "This is just a foretaste if you ever hurt the grease monkey. Got the message?"

Linc wasn't sure whether to laugh or get angry. He settled for being amused. "Roger that."

Steven grinned and Paul smiled broadly right back.

"Roger that," the eldest mimicked and snickered.

"Go easy, Steve. The grease monkey thinks he's okay."

"Yeah well, love doesn't always see straight."

Nevertheless, Steven's elbow and his weight lifted and Linc slowly got to his feet. He rubbed his stomach and turned to face his fiancé's rascally brothers.

Steven was fair haired and built even more powerfully than Paul. His features mirrored their father, where Amelia and Paul looked more like their mother.

Steven grinned and held out his hand. Linc shook it warily. Paul clapped him on the back and indicated the hallway before them that led past a lounge room and bedroom, to what appeared to be a kitchen at the back.

"After you, Linc."

Amusement lurked beneath and he smiled. "If it's all the same to you two, I'd prefer you go first."

Steven and Paul exchanged grins. Paul chuckled and complied with an easy-going gait. Steven picked up the larger of the two bags and followed him. Linc rubbed the back of his neck and wondered what he was in for.

He might have to start watching his back if he couldn't find a way to earn the trust of Amelia's brothers.

He shook his head and trailed the men to the kitchen. The ladies were gathered around the baby in Gwen's arms, while Amelia was sitting across from her father at the small rectangular table.

She looked up when her brothers entered. Her gaze met Linc's uncertain one, swung to her brothers and narrowed. She knew. He watched in amazement as she got up, clipped one across the back of the head and sucker punched the other in the stomach.

He noted that Steven got the punch.

"Take it easy sis'!" he groaned.

Linc was stunned. For someone so shy and small, she obviously packed a wallop. What astonished him more was that her brothers just took it.

"Behave you two or else!"

John snorted in amusement and waved Linc over. "Come take a seat. Gwen will fetch you a cuppa when she's done hugging the baby."

Linc dropped a kiss on Amelia's forehead on his way to the table. "Remind me never to make you mad."

She caught the teasing gleam in his eyes and he watched her blush. She was such a bundle of fire and gentleness that he was again taken aback by what a special person he'd found.

He took her hand and sat in the chair beside hers. As he began a conversation with her father, he knew that whatever her family threw at him, it would never be enough to dissuade him from the precious little woman who had taken over his heart.

45

Several months later:

"Are you going to tell me where we're going?" Nethania got comfortable on the bench inside the wheelhouse of Ollie's boat.

After a detailed police investigation on the island, he finally had it back.

"Longitude one-hundred and forty-eight, latitude sixteen." Ollie gave her an enigmatic smile.

Nethania could not hide her amusement. "And what exactly is so special about longitude one-hundred and forty-eight, latitude sixteen?"

"You'll see. Hey, do you remember Dake Kado?"

Nethania's amused smile evaporated. "How could I forget?"

"The police linked my boat's 'engine trouble' to him. I didn't say anything to you then, but I saw him after we first returned from sea. I didn't know it was him at the time of course. He tailed me for a few weeks and I had him picked up."

Nethania was surprised and a little unnerved. "Do you think he wanted to follow you to the gold?"

"It's possible."

"That's absurd. It's buried at the bottom of the

ocean who knows where."

"Anyway, he was deported when police matched his prints to the ones all over my boat."

Nethania was not altogether surprised. "The love of money..."

"Yeah I know."

Enough time had passed that Nethania was able to forgive and move on. "What happened to the man who shot the Aiji's?"

Ollie studied her carefully before returning his focus to the ocean before them. His right hand draped loosely on the wheel while his left rested on his knee. She finally understood how much he had shielded her from what had happened. He knew every detail, and had kindly kept it to himself when it was obvious she hadn't been ready to face it.

She loved him for it.

"He was found by the feds on the island."

"Dead?"

"Alive, shivering and remorseful. He's in prison awaiting trial. I doubt he'll get out any time soon."

"That's a relief."

Ollie glanced at her in surprise. Had he thought her bitter enough to wish the man dead? Nethania smiled.

"Sin is sin, Ollie. We all get the same penalty before God unless we receive His gift of mercy. I need it just as much as that man does. This way he has a chance to consider his need for God's forgiveness and Christ's sacrifice of love."

Ollie's gaze warmed. "Another reason why I love that

heart of yours."

Nethania's face lit with delight. It wasn't the first time he had told her he loved her, but it never ceased to bring her joy.

Dayne wandered in from the direction of the galley. "Lunch is served you two."

Nethania's eyes danced. "Ooh, what are we having?"

Dayne grimaced. "Cheese toasties. I'm not much of a chef."

"Sounds good enough to me." She rose and trailed him. Ollie cut the engine and followed.

They sat, Dayne gave thanks for the food and they ate.

"Hey, did you tell her where we're going?"

Nethania met Dayne's gaze curiously. "I was told longitude one-hundred and forty-eight, latitude sixteen."

Dayne exchanged glances with Ollie. He looked at her with eyes dancing merrily. "Did he tell you how deep longitude one-hundred and forty-eight, latitude sixteen is?"

"No." Nethania looked between the two of them, now intrigued.

Ollie grinned. "Not very. It's a shallow reef. We sailed right over it that night we fled the island."

Nethania began to piece the puzzle together. Diving gear. A winch on the deck. A secretive exit from port.

Her mind flickered back to the night she had helped Ollie dump the treasure overboard. That last pass through the wheelhouse he had paused by the GPS. Had he memorized the coordinates for a retrieval later?

"Would I be correct in assuming we're not diving to look at coral or fish?"

Ollie winked at her and grinned at Dayne.

"You've picked a sharp one, my friend." Dayne finished his last bite and carried his plate to the sink.

Ollie held her gaze and smiled cheekily. "I sure did."

Nethania wasn't sure what to think. The treasure had brought nothing but trouble since the day it had been brought to the surface during the war.

"What are you planning on doing with the gold?"

Ollie considered her question casually. "Oh I don't know. Maybe a new boat. Dayne wants to buy a house. You might need some funding for your research. Oh, and a few orphanages overseas might need a lifetime of sponsorship."

"You could donate it to a museum," she suggested, reluctant to keep that kind of historical find to themselves.

Dayne smiled at her in amusement. "Do you know how much the finder's fee is for a cache like that?"

Nethania shrugged. "Tell me."

"Enough to do all of that and much more."

She glanced between the two of them in amazement. "You've already looked into this."

Ollie leaned against the bench back. "We even have the museum picked out we're going to call in the find to."

A slow smile parted Nethania's lips. This would be super fun! "Let's go diving boys."

EPILOGUE

Amelia glanced across the bedroom of the quiet country cottage they would be staying in for the next week.

They had decided to tie the knot in Amelia's hometown so that her family and friends could attend. Jaclyn would take Yasmin home to Cairns in a day or so where they would meet her next week. She would stay for the transition and then relocate to a rental home nearby. Apparently the pull of being an aunty was too strong for a move back to Western Australia.

Carrie and Lon had flown down for the occasion, as had Joshua and Joey Donnelly with Faith and their new baby, Michael. It had been a fabulous wedding and reception, one the couple would remember with fondness.

Amelia turned her gaze to the green hills rolling lazily toward the horizon out the window. "I'm nervous."

At her quiet admission, Linc closed the distance between them and his fingers gently brought her chin around. "You're mine for life. There's no rush."

His intimate smile sent spirals of warmth chasing through her. She did not resist, and indeed did not want to, when his lips tenderly claimed hers. They parted and he held her close.

"Love you sir."

Linc caught the cheeky Jones gleam in her eyes and his narrowed. "Don't 'sir' me Teddy."

"Or what?"

He grinned. "Or this." He kissed her again.

She thought that if this was his version of punishment, she would gladly tease him every day for the rest of their lives.

~

Nethania removed her flippers and snorkel and sank onto the pristine white sand. Thanks to their newly acquired funds, her research was flourishing. Ollie's new boat floated at anchor not far from the shore. It almost rivalled The Midas. Dayne had his new house and The Dream Catcher. He seemed to be healing in every way and moving on with life.

Ollie sat beside her and they admired the azure water stretching to the horizon. He glanced sideways.

"I like this place. We'll have to come back some time. What's it called again?"

She smiled back. "I don't think it has a name. It's only a couple of kilometres in circumference. But it's certainly got some fascinating species of coral."

Ollie took her hand in his and held it upon the sand. Nethania gave his a squeeze and enjoyed the perfect moment.

"I could spend a lifetime doing just this."

Nethania glanced at him curiously. "What are you saying?"

"I'm tired of taking you home and saying goodbye to you on your doorstep."

She studied his profile with a hopeful gleam in her amazing eyes. "Me too."

Nethania pretended the same nonchalance he was exuding. "What do you say we do something about it?"

He shrugged. However, it would be impossible to miss the way his hand trembled slightly around hers. "I think that would be a good idea."

"Me too."

His shoulders relaxed and his fear of her saying no evaporated. "What a pain!"

Nethania turned to face him, her face registering astonishment.

He noticed her expression and chuckled. "Sorry, not you. I forgot the ring. It's on the boat."

Nethania laughed and wrapped her arms around his neck. He pulled her onto his lap and sealed the deal with a kiss. She broke contact and pulled him to his feet.

"Where are we going?"

She gathered her gear and headed for the surf. "The boat. I want to see this ring you mentioned."

Ollie watched her trot into the shallow waves. "Seriously?"

She tossed him a grin over her shoulder. "Yes. Now come on!"

He grinned and went after her. Aqua water, a beautiful girl, and a bright future from a loving God. He couldn't imagine anything better.

Dear Reader,

This series has been a fun adventure. The Hartfield's characters feel like old friends, and although I am sad to see them go, you never know what the future may hold. I'm tempted to add more. We'll see.

Although clearly fiction in every way, there were some aspects of this conclusion to the Everyday Heroes series that are true to reality. The most important of these is the depth of relationship a person can have with God.

Linc's character was an interesting one to write. His negative views on God and Christianity, formed by poor models of the faith, are reflective of many people in society who have experienced the same in one form or another.

However, when faced with questions of eternity and Jesus Christ, Linc is finally able to distinguish the difference between imperfect people who identify themselves with Christ, and Christ Himself Who will never fail him. I hope this is so for any readers who may feel just as jaded as he did.

I must admit that I've experienced some of the pain Nethania went through (although not in the form she did), when I watched Christian leaders fall into the trap of judging others wrongly and exercising extreme control. I've seen people hurt, and at times have been hurt, by a lack of love shown by God's people. I too wanted to leave the church, and in fact I did for a couple of months.

The challenge God offered Nethania to love His people, and in doing so love Him, was the challenge He offered me. I returned to church with a renewed attitude, and that very first Sunday back I met my husband. God works in mysterious ways.

I think the thing to remember is that wherever you are, amongst co-workers, friends or family, people are flawed and will let you down. They may mean to, they may not. One way or the other, the result is the same: a wounded heart. I've learned (and am still learning) that forgiveness is a daily act, and that I need God's grace just as much as those who I perceive have hurt me. I too am flawed. I've also learned that I can't offer true forgiveness without Him.

God is able to help you look beyond the hurtful word or deed, to the deeper problems behind it. And always remember, forgiveness is for the one forgiving, not necessarily the one being forgiven. Bitterness is a prison, and at one time or another, we are all in it. God would have us all to walk free of it with His help.

God loves you, and it's not the kind of love a fallible human being will offer. It's unconditional. It's eternal. It's boundless. And it's yours if you'll receive it. The Eternal God is your refuge, and underneath are the everlasting arms. Fall back and let Him catch you. He will never fail you or forsake you.

Whatever point you are at in your journey with God,

from not having started, to many decades along, we all need to be reminded that He loves us. And that He loves everyone else around us just as much. He died for the one spitting in His face as much as the one clinging tearfully to His feet.

These words strike at my heart even as I write them. May God forgive us all for the times we've let Him down, and give us the grace and help we each need to move forward in His love and do better next time.

Love in our very gracious God,

To His Daughter

www.jayhdee.weebly.com

www.ingramcontent.com/pod-product-compliance
Lightning Source LLC
Chambersburg PA
CBHW070632260626
47161CB00007B/2676